SILVER

OVER 100
GREAT NOVELS
OF
EROTIC DOMINATION

If you like one you will probably like the rest

NEW TITLES EVERY MONTH

If you want to be on our confidential mailing list for our Readers' Club Magazine (with extracts from past and forthcoming titles) write to:

SILVER MOON READER SERVICES

Shadowline Publishing Ltd
Box 101
City Business Centre
Stration Rise
York
Y01 6HT
United Kingdom

telephone: 01904 525729
Fax: 01904 522338

NEW AUTHORS WELCOME

Please send submissions to
Silver Moon Books
Box 101
City Business Centre
Stration Rise
York
Y01 6HT

Silver Moon is an imprint of Shadowline Publishing Ltd
the print publishing division of the Convecto Media Group
First published 2008
ISBN 9781-904706-65-6
© 2008 Mark Stewart

JOURNEY INTO SLAVERY

BY

MARK STEWART

In loving memory of my wife

CHAPTER 1.

Melanie was wakened by Julia, her young step-mother-in-law, at seven thirty that Saturday morning. She looked round sleepily for a moment at the unfamiliar room then memory returned. This was the day when her destiny would be fulfilled, when she would take the final steps in her journey to complete slavery. The day of the second 'Wedding Ceremony' when she would again take her vows! But vows that were totally different to those she had taken three weeks earlier in the church where she and Craig, her Master, had been married in accordance with the religious service he had insisted take place.

She had gone through with that ceremony only on the understanding that the second 'Wedding' would be held and the vows taken there to be according to the 'order of service' she had insisted upon. As a consequence of this, her Master had refrained from beating her for three weeks, to ensure that her body would be unmarked for this special event. To relieve Craig of any temptation, she had resided with his father, Alex, and his young second wife since her return the previous Saturday. Craig had desisted from inflicting any corporal punishment on her while they were on honeymoon. He desired that, for the second ceremony to be performed on their return, he wanted her body free from any marks.

With her stomach fluttering at the ordeal that she would soon suffer, Melanie allowed Julia to take charge of her preparation. She was made to eat a light breakfast followed by taking a long hot shower, then Julia supervised her while she sat, naked at the dressing table and applied her make up and her Master's favourite perfume. To complete the preparations, leather cuffs were placed around her wrists and ankles and a soft leather collar round her neck. On the outside of the collar was inscribed in gold lettering the text reading 'I AM THE SLAVE OF MY MASTER, CRAIG WESTON'. The cuffs she knew well. They were part of her normal costume when in Craig's house. The bright rings set into the cuffs had held her restrained whenever she had been flogged in the past. The collar was a new addition to her normal slave's costume that she was to wear, and earn, for the first time. Julia fastened a leather belt around her waist, making sure that the metal rings set into it were correctly placed at her sides so that, as the 'ceremony' progressed, she could be further secured. This, also, was something new, but Melanie had asked for it to ensure that, during the 'ceremony' she was prevented from wriggling too much and spoiling the target she would present. Finally, she was dressed in the tiara, from which a flowing veil was suspended, the one that she had worn at the church ceremony, and which completely covered her body without concealing it. Apart from silver sandals on her feet, beneath this she was completely naked.

As Melanie had asked, ever since she had been woken up, neither girl had spoken to each other except for Julia to give orders, which Melanie obeyed in silence. This was, Melanie had explained, to get her into the right frame of mind. Julia knew the content of the 'Order of Service' that Melanie had insisted upon for the 'Ceremony' and marvelled that she would, of her own choice, subject herself to such an ordeal. But she well knew the girl's wish, and determination that now she was legally Craig's wife, she should still be treated as his slave, only more severely and strictly so.

Alex and Julia were both fully aware of the 'special relationship' between Craig and Melanie. Whilst Alex did, when necessary, impose corporal punishment on Julia it was on the mutual understanding that it was limited, in the number of strokes given at any one time and the force with which they were applied. Also, Julia was only ever beaten across her buttocks. The punishments were administered as between husband and wife. That Craig had inherited his father's philosophy was no surprise, it was only that he had taken it much further, and deeper, into a Master and Slave bonding. That Melanie was utterly happy with this was plain to see and Alex and Julia, although somewhat concerned at first, had come to accept this.

Julia had just finished inspecting the completion of Melanie's preparations when Alex knocked at the door and announced it was time to depart. Julia and Melanie descended the stairs into the hall where Alex, his eyes feasting on the near naked apparition descending, awaited them. He wrapped a huge cloak around Melanie so that, except for her sweet face, she was completely hidden from view. He ushered them out to the car and they set off. On arriving at Craig's house, Alex, using the key Craig had provided, let them enter and ordered Julia to take Melanie to her room where they were to await his summons.

The two girls ascended the stairs and, once in Melanie's bedroom, Julia removed the cloak from Melanie's body and stood looking at her in admiration. Melanie was devastatingly beautiful, made even more so by the fear that now showed in her eyes.

"Are you sure you really want to go through with this?" Julia asked. She could not understand why Melanie, now that she was Craig's wife in the eyes of the law, and everyone else, should have demanded that the slavery she had been subject to up to that time should not only continue but be more rigorously imposed. Julia had agreed with Alex that he could discipline her with a strap, cane or switch across her bottom whenever he thought she deserved it but she had insisted on a limit to the number of strokes she could be made to receive at any one time. She certainly did not subscribe to Melanie's philosophy that a woman should be her man's slave and be treated as such, and willingly submit to whatever he chose to do to her without any limitations of the severity of the thrashings.

"Yes," Melanie answered demurely. "Ever since Craig first spanked me, I have known that, not only was it my destiny to be a slave, but I really needed to be one to be truly happy. I was fortunate that it was the man I fell in love with from the moment I first saw him who became my Master. Now I am his wife as well, it is my wish to take my vows all over again but, this time as his slave."

"It's going to be a terribly agonising way to make your wish to come true," Julia said. She was still concerned at certain parts of the 'Order of Ceremony'. She had seen Melanie badly beaten with the switch by Alex and was aware that she had been punished many times since but was sure the ordeal ahead would be far worse than anything the girl had endured before.

"It is my choice," Melanie replied. "Every part of it! I know it will hurt terribly but, once the pain has gone, I will look back on today and love every moment of the memory of it." Little did Julia know, Melanie thought to herself, of the severity of some of the floggings she had already endured, and loved. The only things that she had not, as yet, experienced were the marking of her body and the implement that would be used on the penultimate part of the ceremony. Those were the things of which she was terrified.

At that moment, the door opened and Jenny, Melanie's sister slave, again dressed in her bridesmaid costume entered. "They are ready for you, Melanie," she announced softly.

"Well, if you're sure," Julia said. "We had better go and get it over with." She picked up a short chain from the bed and attached it to the cuffs on Melanie's wrists. A similar, but longer, chain she attached to the cuffs on her ankles, and clipped a leather lead to the collar around her neck.

Knowing that now was the time she must descend for her ordeal, Melanie picked up a glass from her dressing table and poured some creamy liquid into it.

"What's that you have there?" Julia asked.

"It's a mixture that will ensure that I remain conscious for the next two hours," Melanie replied, quickly quaffing the liquid with a grimace of distaste on her face.

"You mean Craig has ordered that?" Julia asked. Her voice sounded horrified at the idea. She remembered how, on one occasion, Melanie had fainted when Alex had punished her and the horror she felt then when the beating was suspended each time until Melanie had regained consciousness.

"No!" Melanie answered, a nervous smile quivering at the corners of her mouth. "It's my idea and Craig knows nothing of it. I don't want to spoil everything by losing consciousness during the ceremony. I believe it also stimulates the nervous system."

"But that will make the pain even worse!" Julia gasped in horror. "I'll warn Alex and beg him to take things easier this time."

"That you will not!" Melanie nearly shouted. "Please," she added sweetly.

"Alright!" Julia agreed, resigning herself to concurring with Melanie's wishes. She knew better than to argue with her when her mind was made up. "You had better use the bathroom and then, if you are ready, we'd better get a move on. They will be waiting in the Correction Room."

With Jenny holding the back of Melanie's veil and Julia in the rear, the three girls descended the stairs to the hall, and then those to the basement. As she descended the last flight of stairs, Melanie thought that this was the happiest day of her life. She was aware that the temperature was a lot hotter than usual and shivered at what this portended. Outside the Correction Room they halted and Julia knocked

9

at the door. The 'Special Ceremony' that Melanie had choreographed had started. What followed would be in accordance with the script she had written.

"Enter!" Craig's voice boomed from within.

Julia opened the door and entered. "Mrs Melanie Weston desires to enter and take her vows of slavery and submission and receive her Master's mark of ownership," she announced.

"Bring her in."

Although Craig had obviously seen Melanie both naked and dressed in her costume many times before, the vision that entered the room seemed more erotic, and desirable, than ever before. Through the veil, her naked body was enchanting as was the nervous smile on her face as she knelt before him. He glanced sideways to where his father stood and smiled, secretly, at the undisguised look of appreciation on his face. He nodded to his father and returned his gaze to the vision kneeling on the Penitent's Rug in front of him.

"Mrs Melanie Weston," Alex began to read from the script in his hands. "You have expressed the wish to enter into total slavery with Craig Weston as your full Master. Is that your desire still?"

Alex, like Julia, had, at first been reluctant to take part in the proceedings. Not that he disliked the idea of applying the various implements that lay on the table to Melanie's bare behind, nor the fact that, from now on, she was to be treated not as a wife but as a slave. He was aware that, until then, they had been, as he put it to himself, playing at master and slave. After all, it was her own desire and who was he to deny her wishes? What was giving him cause for concern was that, after the vows had been taken, together with the accompanying beatings, her luscious body was to be permanently marked in the most painful manner. He had already assisted Craig in preparing the iron and brazier and the idea of that white hot iron being pressed into her soft and lovely flesh was, to his way of thinking, taking matters too far.

"It is, Sir," Melanie replied, trying to hide the nervousness from sounding in her voice. She felt a shiver pass through her as if her body anticipated the pain shortly to be inflicted on it.

"Rise and take your position," Alex ordered.

At Melanie's request, Craig had installed an old fashioned school desk in the Correction Room. The sloping desk top stood on firm legs that were bolted to the floor. Rising to her feet as seductively as the chains would allow, Melanie walked slowly towards it. She halted so that she was facing her Master seated on the Judgement Seat and with the desk top's slope towards her. Jenny removed the tiara and veil and Melanie mounted the low platform that had been placed in front of the desk and draped her body over it. Jenny was about to attach the rings on the wrist and ankle cuffs to clips at the foot of the legs and thread straps from the side of the desk top through the rings on the belt at her friend's waist, when Melanie rose up and looked at her master.

"Please Master," she said. "To prove my willingness to submit as a true slave, would you permit your slave to remain unsecured to take as many vows as she can without moving. I will beg to be secured when I can take no more."

Craig thought for a moment and then replied. "The slave's request is granted."

Jenny walked away from the desk, collected a bowl of cold water and a cloth and knelt in front of her sister slave, but slightly to one side so as not to obstruct Craig's view.

Melanie draped her body over the desk, holding on to the desk legs as low down as she could reach, and looked sideways at the table on which the implements of her inquisition lay ready. Except for one, none of them were a stranger to her, having already had them laid across all parts of her body, both as punishment and for her Master's pleasure, in the past. She felt a ripple of anticipation flow through her bottom. This was not stretched taut, as it usually was for a beating, as it was necessary for her flesh to be supple for the finale of the question and answer section of the ceremony.

Alex picked up the patterned tawse from the table and moved until he was at Melanie's side. "Look into your Master's eyes and keep them there," he ordered, following the script Melanie had prepared..

Melanie obeyed and saw something strange in Craig's eyes. She did not know if it was love or a little sympathy for the ordeal she was about to undergo. Or could it be anger that she had adamantly insisted on this ceremony before she would consent to become his wife? She had stipulated that it was Alex who would interrogate her, so that she could look into her Master's eyes as she made her vows. She tightened her grip on the desk legs.

"Melanie Weston, do you acknowledge Craig Weston as your Lord and Master?" Alex read from the script. He looked at Melanie's delectable buttocks and, not for the first time, envied his son his ownership of her.

"I do, Sir," Melanie replied, tightening her grip on the legs of the desk even more until her knuckles shone white.

Alex's arm rose and fell ten times, lashing the tawse cross Melanie's buttocks sending a ripple through the cheeks and drawing a stifled gasp from her as each stung her flesh. Her buttocks immediately lost their pale white appearance, turning a bright red. Apart from a gasp each time the tawse landed, Melanie remained silent, concentrating on looking into her Master's eyes. Although it was but a flea bite compared to the beatings she had received in the past, the tawse still hurt like hell as Alex kept his promise to her and laid it on with full force. As she had promised herself, she had not moved as the ten strokes were applied.

After the tenth stroke, Jenny wrung out the cloth and gently wiped it over Melanie's face before wiping away the tears that had seeped from the slave's eyes.

Alex had replaced the tawse on the table and picked up the long rattan cane. Returning to her side, he continued with the questions.

"Melanie Weston. Do you promise to serve your Lord and Master as his slave in all things, at all times and in all ways as he may require?" Alex asked.

"I do, Sir," Melanie replied, silently reminding herself that she must, at least, endure the cane before she begged to be secured.

This time it was the cane that was lashed across her already sore buttocks for the nominated ten strokes. Tears flowed freely from Melanie's eyes and she could not suppress the cries of pain that rose in her throat as each impact sent further waves of fire through her buttocks. She had forgotten the power Alex could put behind the strokes and it took all her mental strength to keep her small hands clamped round the desk legs each time the cane ploughed into her flesh. She must, at all costs, refrain from the natural instinct to rub her behind to ease the pain.

So great was the effort she had to make she almost wished she had asked to be tied from the beginning. But her pride, and determination to show that she suffered willingly, saw her through the ten strokes. At least, she congratulated herself as her cry on the last echoed round the room, she had not moved, nor had she screamed, even though the agony in her behind had reached the stage where another stroke would have broken her resolve. She was grateful for the short hiatus as Jenny bathed her face with the cold cloth.

From where he sat, Craig could see the pain showing in his slave's eyes and face as the beating progressed. He could also see, reflected in the wall mirror behind her, the rod sinking into her buttocks as each stroke was administered. He also saw how the flesh rippled in each impact and the way her cheeks contracted and relaxed spasmodically as she absorbed the pain. Although he knew of her bravery when under discipline, he was amazed that she had not only remained in position so far but that her eyes had, at no time, strayed from his own.

"Keep looking into the eyes of your Master," Alex ordered. Quite unnecessarily, as Melanie's eyes, even though they had filled with tears, had not looked away once so far!

"Mrs Melanie Weston, do you accept your Lord and Master's word as law, never to be questioned?" Alex continued with the questions.

"I do, Sir." Melanie replied, then quickly added. "Please, Master, I beg for my wrists to be secured." She was well aware that it was the birch that would be used on her next and knew that there was no way she could maintain her grip with her hands for even one stroke, especially with the force Alex was laying on the strokes.

She saw Craig lean forward, a proud gleam in his eyes. She prayed he would grant her request. He turned his head and nodded at Jenny. Drinking in his gaze for, what was to be the last time until the questioning finished, Melanie, with a sigh of relief, felt Jenny hasten to secure the cuffs on her wrists to the desk legs. Alex, having replaced the cane with a vicious looking birch, moved to her side.

Melanie had already seen that this was even more terrifying than any other birch that had been used on her in the past and it was that knowledge that had made her beg for her wrists to be secured. She knew, from past experience, that she could endure much more punishment as long as her arms were immobilised.

Alex looked at Melanie's buttocks. Whereas they had been a creamy paleness before the beating started, they were now a dark red all over, due to the tawse, with even darker raised ridges, stretching round both sides of the cheeks, where the cane had dug into her flesh. He raised his arm and brought the birch rods crashing down across the trembling cheeks. Immediately a loud scream echoed round the room and Melanie's buttocks contracted and relaxed rapidly as she absorbed the agony of the stroke. No longer could she keep her eyes fastened on those of her Master as her head shook from side to side with the pain.

Melanie had known she would begin to scream at the first stroke but, she was astounded that her scream was so loud and prolonged. The pain in her buttocks was excruciating. She felt her body begin to sweat and writhe frantically in her bonds, trying to avoid the further strokes that were still to come. Her wrists felt sore where she had struggled to reach behind her to try and rub away the pain. She was glad that her request for her wrists to be secured had been granted.

One by one, Alex laid another nine strokes across the writhing buttocks, wringing loud and long screams from the slave. Her heavily sweating body was writhing frantically and she was thumping her legs so up and down so that her small feet were beating a tattoo on the platform. Alex, and the other two watching, were surprised that, in her struggles to avoid those terrible strokes, she had not fallen off the desk.

Alex went to the table, replaced the birch and picked up a long thin riding switch, one that Melanie had bought for Craig whilst on honeymoon. He returned to the slave's side, carefully inspecting her buttocks as he passed by. He saw that her cheeks were badly swollen, had turned into a deep red with even darker lines where the marks of the cane were turning into vivid bruises. For a moment, he thought of refusing to inflict any more damage on her delightful behind, but he had promised, albeit against his better judgement.

"Melanie Weston. Do you promise to obey your Lord and Master without hesitation or question?" He asked the next question.

"I do, Sir," Melanie managed to say between the sobs that racked her body.

Ten times Alex lashed Melanie's behind with the switch. Each drew an agonised scream from the girl. Her body writhed frantically and her feet drummed loudly on the wooden platform. As the last stroke bit into her cheeks, her body arched rigid with the pain before slumping slackly over the desk top. Tears streamed from her eyes and dropped to the floor to form puddles with the sweat that fell from her nipples.

Melanie thought that her bottom had never hurt so much before. What she had not told Julia was that the potion she had drunk before descending to the Correction Room not only ensured that she remained conscious but also it prohibited any sexual stimulation the beating would create. She did not have this usual distraction to take her mind off the pain she was enduring.

Alex, grateful that his participation in the ceremony was almost at an end, exchanged the switch for the single lash whip. This time, he took up a new position, well to the rear of the sobbing slave.

"Melanie Weston. Do you promise to love your Lord and Master and harbour no affection for any other person?"

"I do, Sir," Melanie stammered. "Please Master, have me secured further." She begged. As Jenny had cleared the tears from her eyes, she had turned her head and seen that Alex had armed himself with the whip. It was another present that she had brought for Craig at the same time as she had bought the switch. It was even more fearsome than the ones he already possessed and she knew it would cut deeper furrows in her tender bottom. Her tender bottom that had already taken forty strokes and she knew she must be fully secured before it began its onslaught on her cheeks or she would surely writhe so much she would fall from the desk.

To her intense relief, Craig must have agreed for she felt Jenny pull her legs apart and clip the rings on her ankle cuffs to rings set at the ends of the platform. To her horror, she realised that this had exposed her sex to the lash. She felt Jenny thread leather straps, which were attached to the sides of the desk top, through the rings in the belt at her waist and pull them tight, forcing her tight down on the desk top. She tried to move and found that she could not even wriggle, so tightly was she held in place.

Having completed the process of securing Melanie, Jenny stepped back and as she passed behind the slave she saw the state of Melanie's bottom and was horrified at the sight. How could the girl take any more punishment? Then she saw the evil whip in Alex's hand. She was tempted to tell the men of the mixture Melanie had drunk and the effect it was having. Perhaps it would induce them either to go easier on her, or to stop the ordeal completely. But although she had not promised and, she knew Melanie wished to see the ceremony through to the end, no matter how bad a state she was in, and decided that, if she spoke out, she would be betraying her friend. So, reluctantly, she resumed her place in front of the shuddering slave.

Craig had watched the performance with mounting pride. He was the owner of this beautiful wench and he visualised the many years ahead. Years of enjoying her body, her expertise in satisfying his sexual needs and the pleasure of beating her body whenever, and however, he desired. He knew his father secretly envied him and wondered how long it would be before he persuaded Julia to submit to him as Melanie had to his son. He signalled Alex to wait a moment or so before continuing, rose and approached Melanie. He walked behind her and inspected her buttocks. The reflection in the mirror had not shown him just how badly bruised she was. Her buttocks had no area which was not covered with weals, those made by the cane and switch showing in hard raised ridges. The surface was not yet sufficiently damaged to mark the white cloth that she had asked be pressed against her bottom after the ordeal was over. But he knew that, if the whip did not do the job, the final implement, which Melanie had designed herself especially for this ceremony, certainly would. Instead of returning to his seat, he stood to one side to closely watch his slave's buttocks as she responded to the two final question sessions.

Alex, standing well back behind the girl, saw Craig give him the signal to proceed. He flicked the lash loose and, with a sudden jerk of his wrist, sent the thong whistling through the sir to send with a sharp report against the trembling buttocks. A shrill scream from Melanie echoed round the room as the lash curled round her bottom. A line of intense fire, overshadowing anything that had gone before, burned in her tender cheeks. As the lash fell away, a thin line of bright red showed where it had fallen and cut the skin. Twice more Alex sent the lash curling round the convulsing buttocks and two more screams echoed the report of the strokes. As the fourth stroke lashed her bottom, Melanie's body arched rigid as she screamed, then collapsed over the desk top. Only the moaning and whimpering that came from her evidenced that she was still conscious as Alex laid the last six strokes across her bottom. The only physical sign of the pain they inflicted was the ripple that spread over her cheeks each time the thong fell away and the increase in the volume of the moans that were issuing from her.

Melanie lay collapsed over the desk, sobbing and

moaning quietly as waves of intense agony flowed through her buttocks. She was glad she had been fully restrained for the whip, although it meant that Alex had an immobile target on which to lay on the lashes. Despite the mist of pain that clouded her brain, she was still conscious, the potion having done its work well and there was no inward signs of the arousal her body usually displayed when she was beaten. But, not having to concentrate on controlling this meant that she had nothing to divert her mind from the pain. Still, she had survived so far and, more important, had not begged for mercy. Now there was only one more question to answer but that would be followed by ten strokes of the dreadful implement she had begged to be used at the end of her ordeal. So far, she was sure, this beating was worse than any she had received up to then.

She shook her head to clear away the mist and heard Alex put down the whip and pick up the dreaded weapon. She felt her buttocks cringing as her behind anticipated what was about to be done to them. She almost wished she had not made the 'paddle' and begged for it to be used on her. She was sure that, even on the first stroke, she would disgrace herself by screaming for mercy or, worse still, lose control of her bladder..

Alex looked hard at the weapon in his hands. It consisted of two pliable strips of leather, glued together, and attached to a wooden handle. It was eighteen inches long with the last twelve inches spreading into two straps, two inches wide. From the surface that would come in contact with her bottom, protruded a number of studs. Alex again looked at the damage he had caused to Melanie's buttocks and the thought of using that final implement on her was too much for him. He walked over to Craig, handed the weapon to him and suggested he, as her Lord and Master, applied the last session. Nodding understanding, Craig took the 'paddle' and stood to one side of his trembling slave.

He looked at her buttocks and saw the lines of bright red where the whip had struck. He understood his father's reluctance to carry on. After all, Julia was no slave and had never endured beatings anywhere as severe as Melanie. Whereas he, Craig, had, unknown to his father, 'owned' several slaves before Melanie and was well acquainted with how much pain a well trained slave could manage. He nodded to his father to continue.

"Melanie Weston. Do you submit yourself to your Master fully and without reservation for as long as he may wish you to do so?" Alex asked the final question.

"I do," Melanie stammered her answer. "Please Master, your slave begs to be gagged." She made her request knowing there was no way she could endure what was to come without begging for mercy.

Craig, suspecting the reason behind the request, nodded his agreement to Jenny.

Jenny, who had watched the thrashing progress with horror at the pain her friend must be enduring also suspected the reason for Melanie's request. Just the very sight of the next implement had made her feel sick with concern for her sister slave. She collected a ball gag from a side table and held it in front of the trussed slave, placing it on her mouth. Melanie, grateful that her plea had been agreed, opened her mouth wide and felt the gag pushed into it and the straps tightened behind her head.

"Slave," Alex announced. "The final implement will be administered by your Master." With obvious relief, Alex read the final line on the script Melanie had prepared. He sat down, carefully avoiding looking at his wife. He wondered what she would have to say to him, once they were alone. Would she be disgusted, angry or just plain ashamed that he had been instrumental in Melanie's suffering? She had sat in silence as she had watched Melanie unmercifully, as she would claim, flogged beyond reasonable limits and heard the girl's screams of agony and seen, reflected in the mirror, the damage that had been caused to the girl's buttocks

Melanie was surprised and pleased at Alex's announcement. All along, she had hoped it would be her Master who would apply the last session, especially as it was to be with that terrible implement. She felt the flat of the 'paddle' thud against her left cheek, and the sharp pain as the studs sank into her soft flesh. Melanie screamed into the gag and, as she knew she would, screamed for mercy. But the gag prevented anyone hearing her disgraceful plea.

Craig looked at his slave's left cheek. Although the whip had created enough damage to satisfy the requirements Melanie had demanded, the studs were ensuring that the job would be well done. The pliable leather, from which the 'paddle' had been made, had curled round the cheek and the studs had sunk in hard. Already, thin lines of red were seeping from the punctures. He had not realised just how effective the 'paddle' would be and regretted having agreed to its use. But she had insisted and, reluctantly, he would keep his promise and deliver the ten strokes she had specified. But, he again resolved, once she had recovered from this morning's work, she would pay for her demands. He raised his arm and continued.

Melanie felt the next stroke landed on her right cheek. Again she screamed for mercy into the gag. Eight more times, alternating between cheeks, Craig lashed the 'paddle' across Melanie's behind. With each, Melanie screamed into the gag. She had not dreamt that the 'paddle' would hurt so much. But, there again, she had not taken into account the damage that would already have been inflicted on her behind. At last, no more strokes landed and she slumped, mewing and moaning, over the desk top.

Jenny, as used as she was to watching Melanie beaten,

sighed with relief when the 'paddle' was pulled free from Melanie's behind after the tenth stroke. She dipped the cloth in the cold water and bathed her sister slave's face. Then she rose and moved behind the girl, first picking up a clean cloth from the table. There was one more task she had to perform. She knelt behind Melanie and shuddered as she got a close up view of the girl's ravaged bottom. As gently as she could, she wiped the cheeks clean of the sweat and blood that covered them. Silently begging her friend's forgiveness, she laid the clean cloth over the beaten buttocks and pressed it hard against the burning flesh. Immediately the cloth was marked with red lines and red dots. She lifted the cloth clear and handed it to Craig.

Julia had watched cringing, as the 'paddle' had been applied to Melanie's buttocks. Whilst she had understood, when the girl had explained to her several years ago that she could only be her natural self when treated as a slave, and that she was lucky that she had fallen deeply in love with the man who had become her master, she could still not comprehend how any girl, no matter how her nature dictated, could ask for, and endure, the ordeal that Melanie had just undergone. She had seen, with her own eyes, the gleam of pleasure in Alex's eyes as he had thrashed Melanie that time with the switch. Again, she had seen the same look, only more pronounced, in his eyes as he had laid on the strokes with the various implements that morning. She just hoped that Alex had not got a desire to mete out such punishment to her. Suppose he demanded that she submit to him, as Melanie had to Craig, as his slave! She hoped not! Or did she? That last thought made her wonder just what lay hidden deep down inside her. Until then, she had accepted limited corporal punishment from Alex. But would she submit, totally, as his slave if he demanded it?

Melanie felt the gag removed and, through tear filled eyes, looked at Jenny kneeling in front of her. "Is it over?"

she asked between sobs. Craig had allowed her five minutes to recover before ordering Jenny to release her.

"Yes," Jenny whispered back as she released Melanie's arms and wrists. She rose and released the girl's ankles and finally removed the strap from round her waist.

Melanie shook her head from side to side to clear away the mist. She was thankful that she had taken the potion and that she had remained conscious throughout the beatings. Her bottom hurt more than it had ever done before and, inwardly, she was ashamed that she had begged for mercy, even though no one had been able to hear her. But she knew her ordeal was not yet over. There was still one more session, the worst she could possibly imagine, to come. Suppressing cries of agony and distress as fresh waves of pain shot through her bottom, she eased herself off the desk and immediately collapsed on the floor. On hands and knees, she crawled to her Master and knelt before him, her knees spread wide. She could not stop the moan of pain that rose in her throat as her heels sank into her throbbing buttocks.

She felt Jenny help her to her feet. Casting a nervous smile at her Master, she turned and gingerly walked slowly to the whipping post and halted with her back to it. Now she must face the worst ordeal of all. Now her young tender thigh was to receive the brand that would mark her as Craig's property for the rest of her life. She trembled violently thinking of the agony this would entail. Craig had wanted to anaesthetise her thigh for this part of the ceremony but she had steadfastly refused.

She watched, apprehensively, as Craig and Alex left the room. Jenny secured her to the post Her wrist cuffs were hands were clipped to rings in the cross piece above her head, then straps were put round her ankles, calves, thighs, hips and waist, and pulled tight, holding her fast against the post. She tried to move but was held completely immobile below her waist. She could feel the post pressing hard into her throbbing buttocks.

Julia quickly walked over to her. "Whatever made you ask for his to be done to you?" she asked softly as she saw Melanie shaking with fear.

"I want to carry the mark of Craig's ownership for the rest of my life," Melanie replied through clenched teeth.

"I think you're very brave and must love him very much." Julia said. "Either that or you're stark raving mad. Please let me go and tell them you have changed your mind."

"No!" Melanie answered through her clenched teeth.

"Please!" Julia begged. "They will not think the worse of you if you do. Your poor body has already suffered more than enough to convince them of your total submission."

Melanie knew that Julia, who was unaccustomed to seeing anyone flogged as hard as she had just been, was only trying to save her from the dreadful agony to come. But she was spared the necessity of answering as Craig and Alex returned. Julia, with a resigned shrug of her shoulders returned to her place.

Melanie felt the strength leave her legs as she saw the men enter the room. Between them they carried a small brazier, filled with white hot coals. It had been the brazier that had made the basement feel unusually warm as she had descended the stairs a while ago. She watched, with mounting terror, as the brazier was set down to the left of her. Craig inspected her bonds to ensure she was securely held and, when he was satisfied, put on a thick pair of leather gloves. Her eyes opened wide in terror as he withdrew an iron from the coals. The end, fashioned like a Gothic letter 'C' glowed white hot. With her terror mounting to the point where she was almost on the verge of taking Julia's advice, she saw the white end in front of her face. Although it was some fifteen inches away, she felt the dreadful heat emanating from it.

"I now mark you as my slave and property." Craig's voice broke the pregnant silence that had filled the room.

The iron dropped low, out of Melanie's vision. She felt the heat near her left thigh.

"I love you, Master!" she called out as she felt the heat grow as it approached her thigh.

Then a sudden searing agony exploded in her thigh as Craig thrust the white hot end into her flesh. Melanie threw back her head and screamed and screamed to the ceiling as the acrid stench of burnt flesh, her flesh, filled her nostrils. She prayed for the oblivion of unconsciousness to descend on her and spare her the agony, but the potion prevented this. Craig, shutting his ears to her screams, pressed the iron deeper into her thigh. After a few seconds, but what seemed like hours to Melanie on the receiving end, he withdrew the iron and returned it to the coals.

Jenny, her face ashen white, feeling sick at the smell of burning flesh, pulled herself together. She had one last task to perform. As soon as the iron was withdrawn, she rushed forward and knelt down at the side of the sobbing girl. As gently as she could, she smoothed antiseptic balm over the wound and strapped a metal gauze mesh over the mark tightening the straps and locking it tight to Melanie's thigh. It was essential to ensure that the mark was not spoiled, to prevent Melanie scratching it until healing was complete.

Once the mesh was in place, Julia and Jenny released the restraining bonds and Melanie subsided to the floor at the base of the post. Although her body was still shaking violently, and heavy sobs were being wrenched from her small frame, the two girls were astounded to see a smile of happiness on her face. Melanie knew that she now carried the mark of her slavery, and Craig's ownership, that he had imprinted on her body and she felt a surge of pride and joy assuage the terrible pain that seared through every part of her young body. Slowly she crawled to the

Judgement Seat where Craig, having with Alex's assistance removed the brazier, had resumed his lace. Stopping in front of him, Melanie gently lowered her body prone to the floor and stretched her arms out sideways.

"Master," she managed to speak clearly through the sobbing. "I thank you for making me your true slave and promise to serve you perfectly for as long as you require me to do so. I thank Alex, Julia and Jenny for assisting in, and witnessing, my submission."

"Rise slave," Craig commanded. "Go and clean yourself and then resume your duties." He was both proud of his ownership of her and the bravery with which she had shown during her ordeal. But he vowed, once again, that, once her body had recovered, she would pay a severe price for blackmailing him into agreeing with her demands. A slave was not permitted to make demands of her Master!

Melanie rose to her feet and, with still trembling legs, hesitantly made her way from the room and up to the bathroom. Jenny followed her and made her stand in the bath while she gently bathed away the signs of the ordeal and applied the cream that Craig had provided and which staunched the bleeding. Afterwards Melanie repaired her make up and brushed out her hair. Then, taking a final look in the mirror at her thigh, she smiled as she saw the angry mark showing through the gauze. She resumed her duties, revelling in the praise she received at the bravery she had displayed in the Correction Room.

The remainder of the day passed and, as soon as Alex and Julia had departed, Craig ordered her to his bedroom where he slaked the sexual desires that had burned in his loins all day. Melanie gave herself freely, ignoring the waves of pain that his taking of her renewed in her buttocks and thighs. He finally gave her permission to come and her body arched as he sent his satisfaction jetting deep into her. Her screams of ecstasy rebounded through the

26

room as a series of shattering orgasms flowed though her, before her body collapsed under him, thoroughly spent. One fleeting thought flashed through her mind before unconsciousness descended on her, and that was, at last, her destiny had been fulfilled.

Craig allowed his slave's body to fully recover before ordering her to the Correction Room to atone for the blackmail she had used on him. A full body whipping was the price he made her pay and, as the lash bit into her back, bottom, breasts and stomach, Jenny was amazed, firstly how the slave's body seemed to move forward, as if welcoming the impact of the thong, and secondly at the smile of happiness that remained throughout the whipping, even remaining in place as she screamed her pain and joy with each stroke of the whip across her tender breasts.

Melanie had, at last, achieved her greatest wish and desire. To be made into the complete and utter slave of the man she loved.

But her journey into slavery had begun four years previously, a week after her twenty-second birthday. A journey which she had taken, painful step by painful step, and which had led to the fulfilment of her desires and dreams. Although the 'ceremony' had been the culmination of many painful, but delicious stages, in her young life, it was, by no means, the end of her journey. She would continue along the road enduring pain and pleasure, beyond the understanding of 'normal women' as they liked to think of themselves, Melanie would not have wished, at any time, to change anything that had happened to her in the past. The pain and pleasure were the substance of her life that made her happier than she would have ever dreamed possible. As sleep slowly overcame her, she remembered each stage of the journey that had begun one Saturday morning four years previously.

CHAPTER 2.

The persistent ringing of the alarm clock woke Melanie at seven o'clock on a Saturday morning. She sleepily reached out her arm and pressed the button that would return the room to silence. As she rubbed the sleep from her eyes to help them focus, it dawned on her that she was naked. She never slept naked! Realisation suddenly invaded her sleep-clouded brain and she sat up with a gasp. Naked? Then she remembered and, with the memory, she felt her stomach begin to flutter with dreadful anticipation. He had ordered her, amongst other things to sleep naked that night.

She eased herself up and sat on the edge of the bed. It was Saturday, a week to the day after her twenty-second birthday. Saturday, the day which, she was to find out, would start her on a journey that would alter her life beyond recognition. A journey into erotic, yet welcome, slavery! As she remembered the other orders he had given her, she felt a fluttering which quickly spread to her vagina. Fear and, yes she had to admit, anticipation sent nervous spasms through her body. She was on the point of letting her hands stray down between her thighs when she stopped. This was not the time to indulge herself!

Turning to the tasks in hand, she made her way into the small kitchen of her flat and prepared herself a light breakfast, followed by a leisurely cigarette, the last she was allowed to smoke before her ordeal. She took a shower, paying particular attention to the private parts of her body, as she had thought of them before becoming involved with Craig. After she had carefully dried herself, she stood in front of a full length mirror in her bedroom and surveyed her body. Not at all bad, she decided. The reflection that looked back at her was of a young woman with a pale creamy white body with fairly wide shoulders that naturally tapered down to a small waist then flared out to a nicely rounded stomach and wide hips. Her breasts were full but firm with well defined areolas and dark prominent nipples. Her legs, which she had always considered her best feature, until Craig had persuaded her otherwise, were long and shapely, having full firm thighs and nicely shaped calves leading down to well turned ankles and small dainty feet.

She turned her back to the mirror and, looking over her shoulder, looked critically at her rear view. Her back was smooth, no sharply protruding shoulder blades, and her bottom was full and firm. She had recently found out that Craig considered her bottom her best feature. He could hardly keep his hands away from it! A shudder ran through her as she thought that the pale virgin 'canvas' of her flesh would soon be marked with the punishment he intended to inflict on it.

She sat at her dressing table mirror and looked at her face. Her green eyes already showed signs of the fear that was building inside her. She shook her head to dispel the fear and applied a seductive body spray over her body. Remembering Craig's preferences and instructions with regard to the use of make up, she began to deal with her face accordingly. She completed her preparations by brushing out her auburn hair until it hung in shining waves to just below the top of her shoulders. A dab of his favourite perfume behind her ears, on her neck and between her breasts complete the task. She regarded the result critically in the mirror with satisfaction. She hoped she would also satisfy Craig's requirements for, to fail to do so would, she was certain, result in serious consequences. There was still a half hour before she must depart and she sat and thought of the events that had led up to her predicament.

She had been immediately attracted to him from the moment she had attended the interview to become his secretary. She had got the job and, as she got to know him better, the attraction had turned into love. Since he had shown no indication that her affection was reciprocated she had kept her thoughts to herself. But two months previously, he had started to take her out to dinner, as a reward for the long hours she spent in the office he said. At first his conduct was exemplary but she soon detected that had found her sexually desirable. She had been more than willing the first time he had seduced her. Then, on the third occasion, he had spanked her before taking her. Although she had struggled, the sex afterwards had been even better. It became the usual thing before each seduction, one time he even used the back of a clothes brush on her bottom. For the first time in her life the word 'submission' came into her mind. There was something about Craig Weston that made her want to obey him, made her want him to give her orders.

But her descent into the world of her dreams had all started, she thought, on the previous Wednesday. During the day, Craig and gone out for a meeting and left her with instructions that she was to contact him on his mobile if a particular client called. The client had called but another girl in the office had felt unwell and had had to have a cab called for her to take her home. By the time everything had been dealt with, the call had gone clean out of her head and it was only when Craig had returned that she had remembered. His face had betrayed his fury but he had kept calm and said nothing, just slamming his door behind him. She was just about to leave for home the following day and was daring to hope that it had passed over when he summoned her to his office. She entered, closing the door behind her and sat in the chair facing his desk. She saw the stern expression on his face and her stomach turned a somersault. She lowered her eyes and awaited his decision as to her future with the firm.

"Yesterday," he began in a serious tone of voice that made her shudder. "You thought fit to deliberately disobey my orders. Disobedience is an offence which I will not tolerate, even from you." He allowed his words to sink into her brain. "I had, initially, intended to dismiss you on the spot. But, on reflection, I have decided to give you another chance. You may choose how I should deal with the matter. Either you can decide to be dismissed, or submit to whatever punishment I decide is appropriate."

As he paused for breath, Melanie raised her eyes and looked into his face, careful to hide the elation she felt. "Punishment? Do you mean you will spank me like you have done before?" she asked, lowering her eyes as she felt her face flush a bright red.

She recalled with a thrill the way he increasingly, as a prelude to sex, pulled her across his knees and, raising her skirt and pulling down her knickers, applied the flat of his hand to her soft bottom. The first time she had struggled and yelled, both with the pain and the indignity of the act until he had paused and stroked her sex lips, immediately finding her clitoris protruding which he tweaked quite hard. The effect had been electric, sending bolts of desire through her loins as a sexual arousal soared through her vagina.

A few more hard slaps to her buttocks and he had dragged her to the bed, and quickly and roughly before she could protest, removed her clothing and thrust her down on the bed. Some women would have described the ensuing sex as nothing more than an assault, until he rolled off her before reaching his climax and began to gently seduce her. The heat of the spanking in her bottom had spread to her belly and, together with the gentle, yet demanding, exploring of his fingers between her labia, had sent her arousal soaring beyond anything she had ever experienced until she had begged him to fuck her again. He had obliged. So satisfyingly and thoroughly that she had ascended into a series of orgasms that had left her utterly drained but totally satisfied. Sex had never before been so wonderful!

The second time, she had not struggled and, although he had spanked her even harder with his hand, and then added a few with the back of a long handled clothes brush, the sex that followed had been far better than the first time. An amused laugh brought dispelled her thoughts, bringing her back to the present.

"I said 'Punishment'" His harsh voice made her look up at him. "Spanking is for fun, as part of the foreplay before sex. By punishment, I mean a sound caning."

"Caning!" Melanie gasped in pretended disbelief. "You mean you intend to cane me on my hands?" She added the last remembering her only experience of corporal punishment whilst at school.

"Not on your hands," Craig replied. "That would be treating you like a schoolgirl. An adult woman is beaten on her backside."

"You mean that you want to take a cane to my bottom?" Melanie asked, not really daring to believe what she had heard. "But that would hurt terribly!"

"Yes. To both questions," Craig replied seriously. "A punishment is meant to hurt, otherwise there would be no lesson learned and, therefore, no point in doing it. So, it's either that or on Friday you can clear your personal things from your desk and leave. A cheque and your cards will be sent to you in the post and we will not see each other ever again." He paused to let her digest his ultimatum. "You have until Saturday to think things over and make up your mind. You will report to my house at ten thirty on Saturday morning. If you do not arrive, I will assume you have accepted your dismissal. In the meantime, this subject will not be discussed further." He then went into a lengthy explanation of what she must do if she decided to accept her punishment.

Melanie left the office and returned to her flat in a daze. She wondered if she had dreamed those minutes in his office, it all seemed so unreal. But it was no dream. It was for real and she had to decide what she would do. Accept the dismissal, or submit to what, she was sure, would be a very painful, not to say humiliating, experience.

Over the next two days it was all she could do to concentrate on her work. Part of her mind was occupied with the problem. Although she was only twenty-two years old, she had had several men friends. Craig, although he was eight years older than her, had proved to be the best lover she had ever had. But it was not only the sex that she found so satisfying. He had, by his self confidence and masterly demeanour, proved to be the only man she would wish to spend the rest of her life with. She could not escape the fact that it was his masterful manner, as well as his handsome looks, that had made her fall madly in love with him. The one drawback was that she did not know if he felt the same way about her. It was not until late Friday afternoon that she made up her mind. She left the office without clearing her desk.

… … …

She looked at the clock on her dressing table and saw that it was ten minutes to ten. She quickly packed her toilet things, perfume and make up in a small overnight bag. She began to dress as he had specified. A gypsy style blouse with an elastic top that she pulled down so that her shoulders, the tops of her breasts were left exposed. Then she put on a wide full-cut skirt that fell only to her knees. To drive there she had decided to wear a pair of flat shoes and, as it was still not very warm outside, a jacket.

She picked up her bag and a pair of silver coloured sandals and made her way down to where her car was parked. As she entered the grounds and brought the car to a halt outside his house, the mixture of fear and excitement that had coursed through her all morning started to increase.

She switched off the engine, removed the jacket and changed the shoes for the sandals. She checked the time on the car clock, he had forbidden her to wear a watch, alighted from the car, locked it and approached the house. She was conscious of the absence of underwear on her body. Feeling very apprehensive, she knocked on the door just as a clock in the hall beyond the door struck the half hour. She heard footsteps and the door opened and Craig stood there, a stern expression on his face.

"Good morning, Sir," Melanie said in a voice tinged with fear and excitement. Normally she only called him 'Sir' in the office but, in the circumstances, she thought it more appropriate to address him in that manner.

"Come in," Craig ordered and when she had obeyed, he closed the door behind her. "Halt and put your bag on the floor."

Melanie obeyed. She shuddered as she felt the rear of her skirt lifted and his hand on her bare bottom, then slide round to her front and delve into her sex. His other hand reached over her shoulder and slipped beneath her blouse and cupped her naked breast, the fingers closing round the nipple. She was not surprised to find that her sex lips were already open and, like the nipple, swollen with the desire his touch immediately generated.

"So you obeyed my orders this time," he said. "Did you follow my other instructions?"

"Yes Sir," Melanie replied, grateful that she had for she would have found it difficult to lie convincingly.

"Leave your bag there and follow me," he ordered.

He led her across the hall, through an archway and into a corridor. He unlocked and opened a door half way along, revealing a flight of steps down. At the foot of the stairs, he halted outside a heavy looking door.

"This is where your punishment will take place. I call it the Correction Room." So saying, he opened the door and ushered her inside. He depressed a switch and immediately the room was flooded with bright light. Melanie looked round the room with horror and could not stop a cry of 'Oh my God' escaping from her mouth at the sight that met her eyes. The room was windowless, one wall covered from floor to ceiling with mirrors, and it resembled pictures she had seen in books of a medieval torture chamber. Chains hung from the ceiling, and scattered round the floor were several items of furniture. Her eyes registered a strongly made wooden rectangular frame, some six feet wide and eight feet high, with chains attached to the corners and along the top, a long wooden bench with a sausage like roll fixed about a third of the way along its length, and a 'T' shaped object which she assumed was a whipping post.

Craig walked towards a thick wooden post about as high as her crotch which had another wooden bar attached horizontally across its top. "This is where you will receive your punishment." He indicated the post. "You will bend over this narrow bar and rest your shoulders on this longer bar, stretching your arms along its length." He pointed to another much longer bar on a post a few feet away from, and slightly lower than, the first.

As he walked towards a side wall, Melanie cast another quick look round and saw various other pieces of furniture whose purpose she could not fathom. She turned her eyes to follow Craig and her heart almost stopped with shock at the array of objects hanging on the wall. He was taking a long thin cane from a hook and was flexing it almost double between his hands.

"This is the cane I will use to punish you with," he continued.

It was not the cane that had shocked Melanie so. She had seen a cane before. It was the other things that hung on the wall. Leather straps, some of which had been split into two or three strips at one end, canes, riding switches

35

and two of three bundles of thin canes tied together which she thought must be birches. Even more shocking were the three whips that hung at the end of the row. Although the thongs were coiled, she could see that they were of varying lengths and thickness. She began to tremble with terror at the very sight of these.

What manner of man, she wondered, would have a room filled with things like this in his house? She realised that this had not just been all put in place for the punishment he intended to give her. She began to see him in a new light and the new image sent shivers of fear, apprehension and happiness through her. He was, if she submitted to him, going to take his domination to the very limit of her endurance. She felt her legs start to go weak. Was that what she wanted? A voice inside her immediately replied that it was!

"Come," he ordered when he thought she had seen enough.

As she turned to follow him, she saw the video cameras placed around the room. He led her up to the hall and into the lounge and ordered her to stand in the centre of the room, facing an armchair on which he sat.

"The beating you are to receive will be in three phases," he announced. "The first phase will be a set number of strokes as punishment for your disobedience. The second phase, which will not be part of the punishment, will be another set number of strokes which I will administer purely for my pleasure."

"You are going to beat me just for the pleasure of it?" Melanie interrupted him aghast as the realisation of what he had said sank into her mind.

"Naturally," Craig responded as if the question was unimportant. "After the second phase, I will allow you fifteen minutes to consider your situation then I will ask you a question. If your answer is 'No' you will be released, allowed to dress and leave this house. We will not, then, see each other ever again. As I have already said, your personal things, cards and a cheque will be sent to you. If your answer is 'Yes', and you have taken the two phases to my satisfaction, I will proceed to phase three."

Melanie was speechless for a moment or two. "What do you mean by 'to your satisfaction'? I will be strapped down and unable to move, after all," she asked eventually.

"I expect a woman to spare my ear drums and take as many strokes as possible in silence and then as many more as she can before starting to scream," was his response.

Melanie shuddered at the word scream. But what more had she expected? She was going to be beaten, it would hurt, and, inevitably she would scream. Surely she should have realised that?

Another question buzzed in her mind. "What is phase three?" she asked, a distinct nervous tremor in her voice.

"Phase three is to determine whether you are suitable material for me to take on as my slave," he replied.

"Slave?" Melanie gasped. Then, forgetting her resolve to pretend to be respectful, asked. "Just what the hell do you mean by that?"

"Exactly what I said," Craig replied. "I have studied you carefully since you became my secretary and have come to the conclusion that, despite your outward appearance of hard headed efficiency, you are very submissive by nature. If you stay with me, either as my secretary or my mistress, it can only be basically as a slave. My slave. You will devote yourself exclusively to the task of serving and pleasing me in all ways, in all things and at all times, without hesitation or question."

Melanie stood silent for some minutes, digesting what he had said and the import of what it meant for her. To her horror, and astonishment, the sheer masterful way in which he had spoken had sent spasms of arousal though her stomach. Not stopping to think whether she was brave enough to concur with his demands, she asked. "If I agree, will you use all those terrible things in that room on me?"

"Of course," he replied. "And not only on those delightful buttocks of yours. Anywhere on your body, from the top of your shoulders to the knees, back and front."

This time, Melanie's silence was more prolonged as the enormity of his words sank in. Involuntarily, her hands had flown to her breasts, almost as if she was trying to protect them from hurt.

Craig sat silent for some time, allowing her to absorb his ultimatum. He wanted her to know, without doubt, exactly what she would be letting herself in for if she submitted. He had taken the plunge and must now wait to find out whether his assessment of her had been correct. Eventually he broke the silence, looking at his watch. "It is now eleven o'clock. You have fifteen minutes to decide. You can leave as I have already said. Or you can strip naked, put these restraints on your wrists and ankles and report to me in the Correction Room." He rose, took some leather restraints from a table behind him, placed them on the chair he had vacated and strode from the room.

Melanie stood where she was for a few minutes, thinking hard. The last thing she wanted was to lose Craig. She was deeply in love with him. But the price for her continued existence with him seemed more than she had anticipated, beyond her belief. She had come there that morning expecting a short, sharp, lesson with a cane. This she had mentally prepared herself to take. Even to submitting to similar treatment in the future, perhaps with things a bit more cruel than a cane. But that was not to be the end of it! She knew that any other sensible girl would just leave, there and then. But she was not just any sensible girl! She was in love with him and was not blind to the fact that she enjoyed the masterful way he treated her. Should she let her heart dictate her course and take the punishment she had brought upon herself and then leave? Her conscience told her that she deserved to atone for her offence.

Or she could follow her heart's desire and stay with him under his terms as his slave. Her intelligence told her that if she did, she would be condemning herself to a life of pain. But there was also the wonderful sex that would, she knew, more than compensate. Did she really love him enough to go through all that, or was it just temporary fascination? Then she recalled the times he had spanked her and how she felt that it was just the natural thing for him to do to her. It came as a bit of a shock to realise she not only enjoyed his mastery, but desired it. Could she ever find another man who would, or could, make her feel the same way? None of the other men she had known had been anything like that with her – more the opposite and that had put her off them.

She looked at the clock on the mantelpiece. The fifteen minutes were nearly up. She had to make her decision. Having weighed all the pros and cons in her mind, she came to a decision. She would stay and try and be the slave he wanted her to be. If it came to the worst, she could always change her mind after phase two! She had better prepare. Then she found that her body had already anticipated her decision, for her hands were already reaching behind her back and releasing the buttons on the blouse. Quickly, she pulled it off and laid it on a chair. The skirt followed as she stepped out of the sandals. She picked up the restraints. They were made of soft leather, with metal rings set into them and a metal clasp to lock them closed.

One by one, she put them round her wrists and ankles. As she locked the last one in place a delicious feeling of vulnerability and submissiveness swept over her, igniting the arousal that had been quietly lurking in her sex since her arrival. After taking the precaution of paying a quick call at the downstairs toilet to empty her bladder, she made her way down the stairs to the basement. She halted outside the door. Her stomach was churning in fear and anticipation and the arousal had begun to escalate.

She ran her hands lightly over her soft and tender bottom, the cheeks of which

would, she had no doubt, soon be burning with agony. She nearly turned and ran but, instead knocked on the door. She heard his command to enter and obeyed, closing the door behind her. She walked as seductively s she could to where he was seated and stopped before him, her eyes firmly fixed on the carpet in front of her.

Craig surveyed the vision standing before him. He had seen her naked often before but, this time, the cuffs on her wrists and ankles seemed to have changed her. She was no longer the self-contained woman she had appeared to be in the past. Now she exuded a mixture of fear and submissiveness. He smiled as he realised he had been right in his assessment of her. But, for his purposes, mere submissiveness was not enough. Was she deeply submissive? Submissive enough to endure the thrashing he was about to give her and, when the time came, a thorough lashing with one of his whips? How would she cope when the lash cut into her tender breasts and between her legs? Time to get on with things!

"If I accept you as a slave." He broke the silence. "There will be a set procedure to be followed when you are summoned to this room. But, as I am sure you wish to get this matter over and done with, we will dispense with that this time. Flagrant disobedience in a slave would warrant a severe lashing with the whip. But, as I have already said, I will content myself this time with applying a severe lesson with the cane across your buttocks. Go and bend over."

Melanie, fighting back the natural instinct to run, turned and walked to the short bar. Now that she had made her decision, she was determined to take the beating well and prove to him that she was made of good slave material, no matter how much it might hurt. She halted when she felt the cool wood against her flesh. She bent over until her shoulders touched the long bar and stretched her arms along its length. For a moment she wondered why she should find herself in such a demeaning position.

She instantly banished these thoughts from her mind and concentrated on what was about to happen to her. She knew why she was there! She was conscious of the subdued whirring of the two video cameras which would record her punishment. She offered no resistance as Craig pulled her feet apart and secured the cuffs on her ankles to rings set in the floor. Those on her wrists he secured to rings at each end of the bar

Immediately the bondage sent shivers down her spine. Now she was completely at his mercy. Bound and naked, a delicious sense of helplessness and submission unexpectedly flowed through her, to be replaced instantly by trembling fear as she looked over her shoulder and saw him take a long, crook handled, cane from one the hooks. As he walked towards where she bent, flexing the supple rattan rod in his hands, she resigned herself to the pain that would shortly sear through her. She had reached the point of no return and must suffer what was to come. She braced herself for the onslaught, steeling herself to try and impress the man she had fallen in love with by taking her punishment as bravely as possible.

Craig stood in front of her and, placing a hand under her chin raised her head until she looked into his eyes. "I have already said that you will not be treated like a schoolgirl. As I have already warned you, the cane will be applied hard. For disobeying my orders, your punishment will be twelve strokes. Then I will apply a further eight strokes which will be solely for my pleasure."

Melanie uttered a gasp of disbelief at the severity of the beating to come and as her mind assessed the extent of the ordeal she was to face. Her poor bottom could not endure such a terrible beating. But he said she was not to be treated as a chid and, if she was to become his slave, what else had she expected? She had never, ever, felt so vulnerable or submissive as she did at that moment. She had made her choice and in her heart she knew this was what she really wanted in life. To be dominated to the very limit of her endurance!

"Just so there is no doubt in your mind, how many strokes does that make?"

"Twenty, Sir." As she mouthed her fate she felt a strong love for him. This was the man she loved and for some inexplicable reason, it suddenly seemed only natural that he should have power such as this over her. After all, it was his dominant demeanour that had mostly attracted her to him.

"Correct. I hope they will instil obedience in you. After that, I will allow you a few minutes to consider your future before asking you the question. Do you understand?"

"Yes, Sir," she managed to stutter. Not just the twelve strokes that had already frightened the life out of her, nor the other eight that would follow them. It was the thought that, if she submitted, she would condemn herself to a further prolonged thrashing to test her suitability. He would continue with the caning until, against her will, he forced her to beg for mercy. How many of those extra strokes would she need to endure before he accepted her as his slave?

After she had felt him secure her wrists and ankles to the table legs, she had expected the beating to commence immediately. Instead she felt his hands glide lightly over her taut cheeks, making her tremble. The unexpected contact made her muscles contract.

"Keep your backside relaxed at all times while you are being beaten," Crag ordered sternly.

Melanie forced her buttocks to relax. Then his other hand reached under her, cupping her breast with the fingers closed on the nipple. A startled gasp came from the bent girl. Then the first hand slipped down, between her legs and pressed against her sex. This time a moan came from her as she felt her clitoris rubbed. The arousal lifted up to another level.

"So!" she heard Craig mutter softly, but loud enough, deliberately, she was sure, for her to hear. "It is not just a mild spanking that arouses her. She is beginning to juice even before I have started. Promising!"

Melanie felt her face turn red with a hot flush. Whilst she had been aware of the fluttering in her stomach and sex, she had not realised that her nipples had become engorged or that her juices had begun to flow. His fingers, still stroking her in those sensitive places, made her needs soar and she was n o the brink of begging him to use her when the fingers, and hand, were removed. Even then, she could not prevent the moan of frustration escaping from her mouth. Then one of his hands gripped her hair again, pulling her face upwards to look into his eyes.

"When I am ready to commence, I will lay the cane lightly on your back. You will ready yourself and then, in a manner appropriate to a slave, acknowledge your offence and beg me to proceed with the punishment, detailing exactly what that is to be."

Melanie, who, as much as she feared the pain to came, wanted nothing more than to get it over and done with, gasped at his order. She was to beg to be flogged! Again, she waited for the first contact of the cane, but it still did not come. Instead she felt his hands on her breasts and sex, rubbing them and making her needs even more demanding. She felt her body instinctively trying to press back against fingers. Then to her dismay, the hands were removed and she felt the cane laid gently on her back.

She steadied her nerves as best as she could and took a deep breath. "Sir, I am guilty of committing the offence of deliberate disobedience and I beg you to punish me with twelve hard strokes of the cane across my bare bottom."

She felt the coolness of the cane lightly touching her soft bottom as he measured his distance for the first stroke. She heard a swishing sound and gripped the bar until her knuckles shone white and clenched her teeth.

Crack.

The report echoed loud in the room and she sucked in her breath as a line of searing agony erupted in her bottom. Her eyes flew open wide in horror at the force of the stroke and she only just managed to stifle the cry of pain and shock that rose in her throat. She had not dreamed that one single stroke of a cane could hurt so much, and that was only the first and she had, at least, another nineteen to come!

Thwack.

Crack.

Two more lines of fire joined the first, the strokes pushing her up onto her toes. Apart from a hiss as she drew air into her lungs between her teeth, she had still managed to remain silent. It was terribly important to her to impress him by taking the beating bravely.

Thwack.

"Aaarrgh!" A short sharp cry was forced from her mouth as the pain in her bottom began to build up and the rigid control she had maintained until then began to snap. Tears flowed from her eyes and fell onto the floor.

Thwack.

"Aarrgh! Aaaaarrrrgggh!" This time the cry was louder and longer as Melanie's body arched with the pain.

Craig paused for a moment, his arm raised ready for the next stroke. He looked at the girl's bottom. Apart from a gasp, and a flinching jerk of her body as each stroke landed, she had remained silent and still for the first three strokes. Now there were five distinct lines where the cane had struck, already turning from the initial whiteness into a bright red. Soon they would change into the familiar tramline signature of a cane. He was impressed by the way she was taking the beating, he had expected her to scream for mercy on the first stroke. A feeling of power and satisfaction surged through him as he watched her buttocks gyrating as she absorbed the strokes.

During his time as a prefect at the public school he had attended, it had fallen upon him to punish the junior boys on various occasions, but he had felt no emotion other than that of knowing they were getting their just desserts. Then, a year or so after leaving school, he had acquired his first 'slave' and he had found that beating her was vastly different. Having a very attractive girl, naked and at his mercy and watching her body writhe delightfully as her buttocks were lashed by the cane had aroused his libido as it had never been roused before. In the twelve years since his school days, he had enjoyed several slaves. But in each case there had been strict limits to the submission he had managed to get out of them.

This was the first time he had availed himself of a female who had agreed to submit without any reservations. There had also been other times when it was not his slave he had thrashed but those had been under circumstances that had precluded him from allowing any pleasure of that nature to be taken from the exercise. But this was different! He was actually living one of his most poignant fantasies. One that had become more frequent since Melanie had joined his firm, and in which she played the starring role. He had found a woman who was prepared, nay wanted, to be taken to the limit of her submission. He shook his head, bringing his mind back to the matter in hand.

Thwack.

"Aaaarrgh!" Melanie again screamed as the supple rod bit into her throbbing bottom, curling round both sides of her soft cheeks..

Craig moved to stand in front of her. He put his hand under her chin, raising her face to his. Floods of tears welled from her eyes and cascaded down her cheeks.

"The lesson is painful, isn't it?" he asked sternly.

"Y…yes S…..Sir," she managed to stammer through her tears.

"You will not do it again, will you?"

"Nnno Sssir."

"So far you have received six strokes." A gasp of disbelief came from the girl at his words. "To ensure that the lesson is well learned, the remaining six strokes of your punishment will be harder."

Melanie had not been counting the strokes. The sheer unaccustomed agony of the beating - except for the times Craig had spanked her as a prelude to sex she had not even been smacked on her bottom before as punishment - had devoured the whole of her mind. The knowledge that she only half way through the punishment phase of her ordeal came as a terrible shock!

Craig resumed his position to her left.

Crack.

Thwack.

Crack.

Another three strokes now flared across the Melanie's buttocks that were now writhing frantically as each added its share of pain to the agony already coursing through her cheeks. Her cries had now turned to screams. Her pale body, which already showed a sheen of perspiration glistening on her skin, heaved with her sobbing in the intervals between each stroke. Still, to his amazement and pleasure, she had not made any overture for mercy or for the flogging to cease.

Thwack.

Crack.

She writhed and squirmed, struggling against her bonds, as the cane laced across her throbbing bottom. Her screams echoed the sharp report of the rattan on her bare flesh. Dark red ridges that were forming on her cheeks now received the full impact of the cane. True to his word, he was laying the cane on much harder now, making the furnace that raged in her bottom escalate beyond her control. Her head jerked from side to side, her ponytail lashing her back, as the waves of agony spread through her whole body. She had lost all contact with her surroundings and was conscious only of the unbelievable pain, whose epicentre was in her buttocks but which had now spread throughout her young body.

Thwack.

Melanie had ceased to struggle as Craig laid the final stoke of phase one across her buttocks. Her only movement was a sharp jerk of her body as the cane bit into her swollen bottom. She continued to scream as successive waves of pain surged through her cheeks, but so far she had not broken down and begged for mercy.

Craig stepped back to survey her buttocks and assess the extent of the damage he had inflicted there. Her once soft cheeks, with their erotic, virgin paleness, were now etched with hard raised ridges that curled round both sides. Tramlines, the distinctive signature of a cane, were already forming on the earlier weals. He was surprised, and secretly pleased, with the unexpected bravery with which she was taking her punishment, considering it was the first time that she had been thrashed on her behind.

He again stood in front of her and raised her face to look at him. "You have now received the twelve strokes of your punishment. You will now have the eight strokes which I will administer for my pleasure. These will, of course, be applied even harder."

Slowly, one by agonising one, the final eight strokes rained down across her buttocks. Her body arched rigid on the first of these before collapsing over the table and one last shrill scream echoed the report. Her body lay immobile as the last five strokes were applied and only a slight jerk and a low moaning and mewing showed she was still conscious of the pain being inflicted on her bottom.

Gradually the agony began to recede as no further strokes were applied. Melanie became aware that her ordeal was over. As the pain began to ebb slightly, she became aware of something else burning in her body. Her belly was on fire, not just from the pain of the beating but from a raging sexual need that had invaded her body.

Craig replaced the cane and stood in front of the thrashed girl. Using her hair again, he raised her face to his and looked into her pain and tear filled eyes.

"I will now leave you for fifteen minutes so that you can consider your future. When I return, I shall ask you if you wish to be tested for slave material." So saying, he left the room, turning off the lights as he went.

Melanie, her bottom still jerking if she were still being struck, lay in the darkness. Her bottom hurt more than she had ever dreamed possible. It felt as if she had been made to sit on glowing coals. Slowly she forced herself under control and her breathing gradually returned to normal. Soft moans and mewing still sounded in the room as waves of pain continued to flow through her buttocks. She had expected a bad beating but had not thought it would be as bad as it had been. Yet, although she had screamed, she had managed, much to her surprise, to stay silent for the first three strokes and she had not begged for mercy.

Through the mist of pain that clouded her eyes, she had

heard his words with some relief. At least the first two phases, as he had called them, were over and she had survived. Not only that but, since he had not released her, she must have taken them to his satisfaction. Now she had to decide whether to cause further pain to be inflicted on her bottom and prolong the agony, with all that that would entail for the future, or to call a halt and lose him for ever. She shook her head to clear her mind and tried to concentrate her thoughts on the question. Back and forth in her mind, went the argument for and against – many more points for than against as it turned out. As she considered each, she always ended up at the same point.

She knew she was deeply in love with Craig, if misery at the prospect of never seeing him again was love. The sex with him had been so out of this world, as the mind shattering orgasms he induced in her proved, that she could not envisage being without it. None of her previous encounters could hold a candle to him as a lover! His masterful attitude was another thing that attracted her strongly. She had never, until she had met him, considered herself at all submissive but, with him, it seemed so natural. Not only that, but she enjoyed the submissive feelings he aroused in her. Even during the caning she had just received, she had never once felt anything but love for him. In fact, the pain seemed to emphasise that love.

She was still deliberating the issue when the door opened and the lights were switched on again. She looked over her shoulder and, through eyes that were still misty with tears, saw that he had changed into his silk dressing gown. She wondered why. Was he naked beneath? The very thought stirred the arousal in her belly. She turned her head to the front and waited for the question he would ask her.

But instead of the question, she felt pressure against her sex. Without any preliminaries, he thrust his rampant penis deep into her tunnel. He commenced to slake his thirst on her, pumping in and out vigorously, sending her arousal soaring. He was clearly not interested in giving any thought to either her comfort or desires, although the ease with which he had penetrated her must have told him that she was fully aroused and ready for him.

He came to his climax with cry of pleasure and satisfaction as he jetted his sperm deep into her. It was but a few seconds after that Melanie's body arched and she screamed with pleasure as she succumbed to a series of the most shattering orgasms she had ever enjoyed. As she slowly surfaced to consciousness, her mind no longer debated the problem. It had been made up for her. His arrogant taking of her had banished any doubts as to what her answer to the question would be.

She didn't wait for the question. "Please make me your slave, Craig!" she called out. "I love you. Test me as much as you wish and I will prove worthy of the honour."

Melanie had made her decision and now the die was cast. She had committed herself to him for as long as he wanted her. Now all she had to do was persuade him to lead her into slavery. In silence, she waited for his reply, but none came. She wanted the third phase to commence so she could prove that she was capable of meeting any standards he might set for her.

Thwack.

Without any warning the cane lashed her already pain-ravaged buttocks as she entered into phase three of her ordeal. Her scream of pain and surprise echoed the report of the stroke. Her lips were drawn back over her teeth in a grimace of utter agony as the fire in her bottom received more fuel to stoke it further. Through the fog of pain, she wondered if that stroke had been harder that any of the previous ones. The next stroke convinced her that it had! He really was intending to test her powers of endurance and control.

Stroke after stroke rained down on her gyrating buttocks, each adding to the white hot furnace that blazed in her cheeks. Each drew an agonised scream of pain from her throat until she was unable to cry out any more. The strength had evaporated from her and she lay motionless across the bars, only a jerk of her body, and the ripple that flowed across her cheeks each time the cane bit into her bruised bottom, showed that she was still conscious and aware of the thrashing being dealt out to her. The arousal, that his taking of her had ignited and which had only begun to subside, flared up again and she knew she did not have any strength left to control it. It was only when she feared that she would lose consciousness, either from the pain of the beating or the orgasm that she knew was imminent, that she finally found enough breath and strength to screamed for mercy. For the beating to stop!

Craig halted the stroke that was about to descend as he heard her plea. He went behind her and looked at her buttocks. They were badly swollen, bruised all over and a mass of hard ridges stood out from the surface, and, due to the flexibility of the cane, they curled round both sides of her cheeks.

He went and stood in front of her and, again raised her head. "So that you fully understand that a Master takes no heed of a slave's cries for mercy, I will give you another six strokes." He resumed his position and kept his word.

He returned the cane to its hook and resumed his seat. He looked at Melanie and was amazed that she had taken so many strokes in phase three before capitulating. She was sobbing quietly and her body was still shuddering. Her buttocks continued to clench and relax spasmodically in an attempt to ease the pain ravaging them. He allowed her a few minutes before releasing her limbs and ordering her to go to the bathroom and attend to her appearance before reporting to him in the lounge.

CHAPTER 3.

Melanie had felt the bonds released and had collapsed in a sobbing heap on the floor. She heard Craig's order. Slowly she rose and, treading gingerly, left the room. As soon as she was outside the door, her small hands flew to her bottom to ease the pain. She was astounded at the heat that radiated from her cheeks. Her fingers felt the hard ridges left by the cane on her soft flesh. Mounting the stairs sent fresh waves of pain through her bottom. She found the bathroom, and the first thing she did when was to inspect her bottom in the mirror. She uttered a gasp of horror at the sight that met her eyes. Her once pale cheeks were a mass of hard dark red weals on a bed of blue bruises. There was nowhere where the original whiteness still showed. Even both sides of her cheeks were as bad as the rest, showing where the supple cane had wrapped round her. In some places the skin had broken and thin bright red lines shone along the worst of the weals. She had been well and truly thrashed!

A few hours earlier, she would never have believed that her soft and tender bottom could endure such a terrible beating. But, far from hating Craig for the damage he had done to her, she had to concede that he had only behaved as a master would do towards his slave. Also, it was her own fault, she had to admit.

While she was attending to herself, Craig had seated himself in a comfortable armchair in the lounge. He had been pleasantly surprised, or more accurately astounded, at the way Melanie had endured the thrashing. He had not expected her to take even the first twelve strokes before begging for mercy. She had not only taken those and the eight he had laid on for his pleasure, but another ten of the hardest he could lay on before her scream for mercy had been forced from her.

Then there had been those six strokes he had added to

teach her that a master takes no notice of a slave's plea for mercy. Thirty six strokes for a first meeting with a cane, or any other implement, was well beyond his expectations, or experience with previous slaves. He congratulated himself on his accurate assessment of her. He had gained quite a lot of experience with his previous slaves and it was not long after he had engaged her as his secretary that he had sensed a hidden submissiveness in her. He had covertly watched her as she went about her duties. He had taken particular interest in the views he had been treated to of her buttocks. Even through her clothes, they were very appetising, and he had often thought of the pleasure he could enjoy with them at his mercy. This morning's display foretold a very entertaining and enjoyable future. He might even keep her, instead of selling her on, as he had disposed of his other slaves when he tired of them.

His thoughts were interrupted by a knock on the door. On his command, Melanie entered and walked to him, halting a few feet away. Without thinking, she dropped gracefully to her knees, keeping them spread wide and placed her hands, palms down, on the carpet at her side. She kept her eyes demurely lowered.

Craig smiled with satisfaction at the manner of her approach. It was exactly how he would have expected a trained slave to behave, and he hadn't even started her training. "I trust that your punishment will be a lesson in obedience," he said, forcing his voice to be stern and not betray the intense pleasure he had enjoyed that afternoon.

"Yes, Master," Melanie replied automatically. "Thank you for my beating."

Craig smiled at her calling him Master before he had announced his decision to take her as his slave. "A very painful way of learning a lesson!" he said. "Your bottom must hurt a lot."

"It feels as if I'm sitting on hot coals, Master," Melanie

replied, again referring to him as 'Master'. It just seemed a natural thing to do!

"You referred to me as 'Sir' before the punishment and then by my name when I was using you, afterwards and now, again, you have called me 'Master'. Why?"

"When I entered the house, I thought it prudent to be respectful and call you 'Sir' as if we were in the office. When I called you by name, I was not thinking properly. I had such demanding needs raging through me, all I could think about was begging you to soothe them. Then, afterwards, it seemed natural to call you 'Master'. Being tied down naked and beaten, and then the masterful way you took me, I felt more like a slave girl who was at the mercy of her master rather than your secretary. I hope I have been sufficiently pleasing to be accepted as your slave," Melanie replied.

"Yes," he said, trying to keep his voice sounding normal. "While you were upstairs, I have been thinking. With immediate effect, you will continue with your secretarial duties, but there will be a change in your job specification," he announced sternly.

"Do you mean that I have passed the test?" Melanie asked, not trying to hide her assumption that she had, and the happiness she felt at the prospect.

"Yes," Craig replied. "Just now you said that you felt like a slave and that is what you will be from now on. My slave in the full meaning of the word, with no conditions attached to your submission! You will give up your flat and move in here and serve me as such."

"You accept me to be your slave, Master?" Melanie asked, raising her eyes and letting him see the smile of happiness on her face. "I promise to totally submit to your will, and be owned by you, I am yours to do with as you please." She bent her body over until her forehead touched the floor.

"Correct!" Craig replied. "You will submit to me at all times, both in and out of the office. In the office, and when we are otherwise away from this house, you will refer to me as 'Sir' at all times unless I inform you otherwise. You understand?"

"Yes, Master."

"You will dispense with bras, knickers, stockings and tights at all times away from this house, to remind you that, while you do not call me Master, you are still a slave. In the house, you will either wear a garment I will choose for you or be naked."

"Yes, Master," she said, "I submit myself to you as your slave. I am yours to do with as you wish." She repeated her words of submission.

Craig looked down on her luscious body, the body that, by her declaration, he now owned. From the moment she had entered the house that morning, he had felt his libido rising. His taking of her had been quick and domineering but had not fully quenched his desires. He felt his manhood stiffen. He ordered her to rise. His eyes devoured her, pure lust making them shine. He signalled her to turn round, which she did. He surveyed her delightful bottom, which bore the marks of her punishment. The marks of his ownership! The sight fuelled his desires and he ordered her to face him and kneel.

For some unknown reason, Melanie no longer felt awkward, being naked before him. In speaking her submission, she had banished the feeling of embarrassment that had simmered in her mind since she had entered his house. Her lowered eyes noticed the bulge in his trousers and, without thinking, she knelt and reached forward and undid his flies and her fingers released his lance from the constriction of his clothing. It was engorged, the crown purple with his desire, and the slit was open, leaking a tear of his desire. More by instinct than anything else, she leaned forward and kissed the throbbing crown. Although she was no virgin, she had never even handled a man's penis before, not even his and certainly had never had her face so close to one. It seemed only natural for her to open her lips and take the staff of her master into her mouth.

For the first time in her life, she tasted the saltiness of a man's desire. She began to caress it with her tongue, sensing the blood surging through it as she stimulated his needs. Suddenly, her head was thrust away from him. Had she done something wrong? Before she could decide, he pushed her to the floor, spread her legs, and thrust his shaft deep into her vagina. This time, he was more leisurely in his taking of her. Despite the aggravation of the pain in her buttocks as she writhed on the carpet, Melanie felt her own body responding as an orgasm rose in her. She felt the rhythm of his thrusting increase and, just as he jettisoned his juices into her for the second time, her body arched under him until only her head and heels touched the floor.

As a series of shattering orgasms raged through her body, a shrill scream of erotic satisfaction issued from her open mouth as she yelled, "Master. Master, I am your slave!", over and over again. Just as she descended into a dark void, she had time to wonder what the future held for her and to what she had condemned herself.

Many times in the future, Melanie was to think back to that Saturday and of the way her life had been changed. Until then, she had treated her various boyfriends with a veiled contempt. Why, she did not know, it just seemed the right way to behave. However, on entering Craig's employment, she had felt that there was something different about him. His quiet masculinity, and the subtle aura of dominance that he exuded, made her realise that she could not treat him like the others. That she had fallen in love with him had come as somewhat of a shock. That Saturday had awakened something inside her that had lain latent.

She had agreed to the caning merely to keep her job and stay near him. Yet, as the cane had lashed her buttocks, she had learned that she was not the girl she thought she was. She had learned the wonderful feeling of submission.

The following Saturday, she moved into Craig's home. The house was quite large, much larger than she had initially thought and he had made provision for her accommodation. The door to her bedroom had been removed, as had the door to an en suite shower and toilet, as he maintained that a slave had no rights of privacy. He showed her over the remainder of the house, except the Correction Room, which she had already encountered, and explained her duties as a slave as he went.

The tour of the house completed, he led her into the lounge where he ordered her to kneel in front of him. Continuing to inform her of her duties, he informed her that he would expect perfect behaviour from her and that, where her common sense and imagination failed to tell her the manner in which a slave should conduct herself, painful education certainly would.

She was to remain silent at all times unless he spoke to her. If she wished to speak, she must first ask permission. She must keep her eyes demurely lowered at all times in his presence and, unless she was performing some task, she was to kneel in his presence, with her knees together and her hands placed, palms down, on the floor at her side. If she was naked, her heels must be close together but her knees spread wide apart.

As he had already intimated he would, he informed her that, when in the house, she would wear only one of several very transparent negligees which he had purchased and she would find in her room. When he so ordered she would be naked and, when she had been punished, she had to remain naked for the remainder of the day and display the marks of his displeasure.

Melanie digested this with a mixture of pride and pleasure. She knew her body was, as he had told her several times, a sight worth looking at. She already felt an element of pride in the marks of his ownership that her body already carried. But his words brought questions that, she had to ask, although she dreaded what the answers would be

"Permission to speak, Master?" she asked.

"Speak!"

"What do I do if you have visitors?"

"Then you will be given one of three orders. First, to go to your room and stay there until I summon you after they have gone. Second, I will order you to go and quickly change into a skirt and blouse and continue in their presence as if you were merely my mistress. But remember, if you step out of line while they are here, you will be punished, understand?"

"Yes, Master," Melanie replied then, fearfully, added. "And the third order, Master?"

"The third order will be to continue with your duties as a slave."

"Even if I am naked?"

"Certainly, why not?"

"But, if I have been beaten, they will see the marks on my body." Whilst, she was proud to bear them, and for him so see, she cringed at the thought of strangers having the same views! Also, it would mean that what she had hoped would always be a secret between the two of them would become common knowledge.

"If they can see that you are a slave, it will not come as a surprise to them if it has been necessary to punish you," Craig responded sternly. "But, be assured. Only those whom I can trust not to speak of the matter outside this house, will be given that privilege."

Melanie was somewhat reassured by his reply but his answer led to further doubts in her mind. "If they can see

58

that I am beaten," she continued, risking his anger at more questions. "Will you order me to take a beating in front of others, or to submit to others beating me?" Then, before Craig could answer, continued. "Will I be ordered to submit sexually to anyone other than you?"

"Yes, if I consider it desirable, is the answer to the first two questions," Craig replied. "As to the third question, your body is mine and it would not be my wish to share it with others, unless circumstances require it. But, if anyone, man or woman, becomes sexually uncomfortable through arousal at seeing you naked, or beaten, I will order you to relieve their discomfort with your hands and mouth."

Inwardly Melanie breathed a sigh of relief. He wanted to keep her body to himself, except in special circumstances. That she would have to satisfy them with her fingers and mouth was to be expected, although she shuddered at the thought of having to service another woman in that manner. She had never even thought of doing such a thing before! But she was now a slave and must obey his demands! That he clearly intended her to be thoroughly dominated made her feel proud and happy. There would be no half measures in her submission!

Her silence following his disclosure indicating that she had no more questions, he continued with her instruction. He reminded her that underwear of any kind was banned at all times outside the house, even in the office, but allowed that she might wear a longer skirt to protect her modesty. As time passed, she often wondered what the other employees and the people she met, day by day, would think if they knew, especially when her bottom had been decorated by one of those dreaded implements. But she revelled in her secret.

From then on, Melanie soon settled in to her new role. As he had promised, he became a strict disciplinarian, and ruled her, both at home and in the office, with a rod of iron. Consequently, her visits to the Correction Room were to become frequent and she was never to leave there without her bottom in a painful condition.

Several months passed and Melanie felt happier than she had ever been before. She attended to her office duties with more diligence and, in the house cooked and cleaned with equal attention. But she was not perfect and her bottom paid the price. As he had said, painful education soon saw her visiting the Correction Room to be punished less frequently. But, in between times, she was still was summoned there to be beaten for his pleasure. On these occasions, she looked at the reflection of her bruised buttocks with extra pride. She was fulfilling her duty to her Master and giving him pleasure.

But her life was not just work and beatings. Craig frequently took her out for meals or to visit the theatre. Occasionally, when he had to undertake a business trip, he ordered her to accompany him. There was always a cane, tawse and gag in his luggage and he did not hesitate to make use of these in the solitude of their hotel room, with the sound on the T.V. turned up somewhat to mask the sounds of impact against her bare flesh. The beatings, then, were not severe. Just sufficient to add spice to the sex that followed!

The one thing that kept recurring in Melanie's mind however, was that Craig had refrained from hitting her anywhere other than on her buttocks and he had not used any of the whips on her that decorated the Correction Room wall. She was both relieved and disappointed at this. Relieved because she feared the pain she would suffer – disappointed because she felt that, until she suffered the lash on her back, she would not be a true slave, either in her or his eyes.

Visitors to the house were rare, except for Craig's father and his young second wife, Julia. During these times, she was allowed to wear a dress or skirt and blouse. Julia was five years older than Melanie, with long auburn hair, shapely legs and a figure that completely belied the fact that she had a two year old son. Melanie found it hard to play the part of Craig's mistress when, in her heart, she knew she was a slave. Still, with an extra effort, she managed to keep up the pretence, ensuring that her behaviour was above criticism from her Master after the guests had departed. Julia and her husband were, to Melanie's relief, kept ignorant of her true status. That was until one fateful day some eight months after her declaration of submission when her secret slave status ceased to exist as far as they were concerned.

Alex and Julia had called and a game of bridge was in progress. The evening had taken its usual course, the game was nearing its conclusion and the scores were, unusually, even. Hence, the game had become very exciting. Melanie was partnering Alex when, in a moment of aberration, she made a fateful mistake. She played a trump on his trick.

"That was a stupid thing to do!" Alex exploded, looking at her, his face reddening with anger at losing the hand.

"Not as stupid as leading hearts when you should have known it was my bare suit, you idiot!" Melanie shouted back in the heat of the moment, completely forgetting that she was, as a slave, expected to be respectful at all times.

As happens when tensions run high, a heated argument began between the two until Craig ordered her, in no uncertain terms, to 'hold her tongue'. However, by then, the damage had been done. Matters calmed down and the evening drew to a conclusion without any further incidents. After Alex and Julia had departed, Craig, as she had expected once she had cooled down, took her to task. She knew she had overstepped the mark and would undoubtedly be punished for her rudeness. The duty of a slave, he had dinned into her, was to show respect at all times, irrespective of any provocation. What she was not prepared for was the order she was given.

She was to go to Alex's office the next morning, and apologise to him. She was also to explain, in detail, her true relationship with Craig and to inform him that she was to be punished for her behaviour the following Saturday afternoon. The bombshell came when Craig ordered her to invite Alex and Julia to be present and witness her beating.

Melanie was aghast at his orders. Their secret relationship was to be shared, something she had never expected to happen, despite Craig's warning on her first day in his house. Not only share the secret, they were to actually witness her being beaten!

Melanie's persistent pleading against his judgement was in vain. Craig insisted that, in that incident, justice must not only be done but must be seen to be done and, as Alex and Julia were the victims of her crime, it was therefore necessary for them to witness justice being carried out. Consequently, because it was his orders and she must obey or make matters worse for herself, she spent a very embarrassing half-hour or so closeted with Alex in his office. Not daring to omit anything, in case Craig checked up on her, she told him all, exactly according to Craig's instructions. Alex heard her out without interruption, although she did notice his eyebrows rise when she explained her slave status. But, on hearing of the invitation, he accepted without asking any questions. This completely baffled Melanie since she had assumed that he would be astounded by her revelation that his son intended to thrash her.

On Saturday, Melanie woke with a feeling of doom hanging over her. Although she was always apprehensive when waiting to present herself in the Correction Room she willingly accepted her visits there as a way of life. She still feared the pain she suffered there, but the sexual stimulation that always seemed to surge through her as the punishment progressed quickly made the beatings bearable and also, welcome. The happiness she enjoyed the rest of the time, due to her submission to Craig as her master, made those ordeals more than worthwhile. After all, that degree of submission was necessary for her happiness to be complete. Not only that, each time she suffered, she knew she was giving her master the pleasure he desired. But this day was to be a real test of her submission. Not only were Alex and Julia to be present but, on her return from Alex's office, Craig had ordered that when her punishment was announced on the day, and not beforehand, she was to ask Alex to administer the punishment. How she would react to being beaten by someone other than Craig she did not know. Ever since he had given that order she had tried to banish the thought from her mind.

The morning passed slowly, her apprehension increasing by the minute. After an early lunch, during which she found it difficult to eat anything, she excused herself and went upstairs to prepare. A quick bath then she applied her make up and brushed her hair until it hung in a shining cascade to between her shoulder blades. Finally, when she was sure her appearance was perfect, she put on her negligee. It was black and of the finest material which did little or nothing to conceal her naked charms. She descended to the lounge and. after submitting to a critical inspection from Craig, awaited the arrival of the guests.

She heard the car come up the drive and went to wait by the front door, her legs shaking in trepidation. Trying her hardest to hide her feelings, she admitted Alex and Julia and greeted them in a manner befitting a slave.

"Greetings, Sir. Greetings, Madam," Melanie said, as demurely as she could, keeping her eyes submissively lowered. "The Master is awaiting you in the lounge. Please follow me." She led them into the lounge and announced their arrival to her Master.

Craig greeted his father and stepmother as if nothing untoward was to happen. He then ordered Melanie to go and prepare coffee for him and the guests. Alex carried a parcel under his arm, which he handed to Craig before seating himself.

Thankful to get away from the admiring glances that Alex kept directing at her, Melanie made her way to the kitchen. She began to prepare the refreshments. Now that the time had come, she suddenly realised that she was more frightened than normal. It was not the beating that she feared, she was by then well used to punishments. It was the presence of witnesses, and the knowledge that they would probably see her body's sexual reaction to the pain that unnerved her. Also, she was to be beaten by another man and that brought tears of embarrassment to her eyes. She suddenly sensed the presence of another in the kitchen and turned to find Julia standing in the doorway.

"Is there something I can do for you, Madam?" she asked demurely, brushing a tear from her eye.

"I've come to see if I can help you," Julia responded gently. "And you can forget the 'Madam' bit when we are alone."

"I daren't. If my Master heard, I would be in even more trouble." Melanie could not hide the fear from her voice.

"Alex has told me why we are here and of the true relationship between you and Craig," Julia said softly, approaching Melanie and putting a comforting arm round her shoulders. "The men are busy discussing your fate, so they won't hear us. You must try and be brave and hide your tears, it will spoil your make up." She hugged Melanie tighter. "Come on love. It'll soon be over."

"It's alright for you," Melanie whispered. "You and Alex are going to see me stripped naked and beaten. You have

64

no idea what it is like just to be beaten, let alone have to take it, naked, in front of witnesses."

"That's what you think." Julia responded. She stepped back, turned, and raised the skirt of her dress and lowered her knickers. Melanie stared in disbelief at the exposed bottom. Dark red lines edged by bruising covered both cheeks, obviously made by the forceful application of a rod of some sort.

"I got that last Saturday, twelve with the cane for arguing with Alex. Surely you didn't think you were the only one to be treated in that way? Where do you think Craig got the idea from? He's just taken things much further with this slave business."

As Julia adjusted her dress, Melanie shook her head in wonder and terror. The beating had been done last Saturday, a week ago, yet the weals still looked horribly fresh. She trembled as she imagined the force Alex must have used.

"Just be thankful that it's Craig and not Alex that will be beating you," Julia added as she turned back to face Melanie. "He doesn't lay it on so hard."

"How would you know?" Melanie asked, startled by the girl's remark.

"Last year Alex injured his right wrist and, rather than let my punishments mount up, he got Craig to do it for him. If I am to be beaten, I would rather bend for Craig than Alex any day."

"Oh my God!" Melanie could not help the words slipping out. She began to shake visibly. That a mere twelve strokes of a cane could leave such marks, which were already a week old, attested to the force with which they must have been applied.

"Whatever's the matter?" Julia asked, concerned at the look of terror that had appeared on Melanie's face.

"You mustn't let on that I've told you," Melanie stammered. "I've been ordered to invite Alex to administer my punishment." Her voice had dropped to a terrified whisper. "Craig is really angry with me. I know that he considers my offence to be of the utmost seriousness and I'm sure that I'll be whipped, and it'll be my first time. I've seen the force Alex must have used when he caned you last Saturday, the marks still look fresh even after a week and I'm terrified."

"You can stop fretting about that," Julia tried to reassure her. "I can tell you that it is not a whip they are considering for your punishment."

The two girls took the coffee and biscuits through into the lounge. As she served the refreshments, Melanie did not fail to notice the Record Book, open between the two men. The book in which every punishment that she had ever received was recorded. There were entries showing she had felt the strap, the tawse and the cane, together with the offences she had committed. She wondered what entry would be made for the punishment she was about to receive. If Julia was right, at least it would not be a whip, as she had feared would feature there. She completed her task and bowing respectfully, retreated to the sanctuary of the kitchen. Fifteen agonising minutes dragged by before Julia reappeared.

"They have decided, but I am not allowed to tell you," Julia announced. "I have, however, been told to explain to you what's meant by 'Punishment Discipline' as Alex calls it when my offence stems from lack of self control. Sometimes when I am punished I am put under Punishment Discipline. This means that at the commencement of the beating, I am ordered to take a specified number of strokes in complete silence. This makes me exert rigid self-control and is to teach me why I am being punished. If I make a sound at any time during this period, the specified number of strokes is added to my punishment. If 'Double Punishment Discipline' is ordered, and I fail, then the number of penalty strokes is doubled. Alex says it helps to drive the lesson home. This afternoon, you are to be put under the same discipline."

"That's terrible," Melanie whispered, her voice trembling with fear. "I always try to take the beatings bravely and Craig has never stopped me from crying out. I could never stay silent, even if he ordered me to!"

"It will be a terrible ordeal, but you must try as hard as you can," Julia said softly. "As it's your first time, I've managed to persuade Alex to let me help you by warning you when the stroke is coming and counting them out loud." She then explained what had been agreed.

"Thank you, Julia," Melanie said hugging her friend. "That will be some help at least."

"Now I must rejoin the men." Julia disengaged herself from Melanie's embrace. As she reached the door she turned. "You are to report to the Correction Room in ten minutes, at three o'clock sharp. Good luck!"

Melanie used the intervening minutes to try and compose herself, but the sight of Julia's bottom, a week after the caning, had unnerved her. If Alex used the same amount of force when he beat her, and Craig had said she must stipulate that he show her no mercy, she shuddered to think what her bottom would look like, not to mention the agony she would have to endure to get that far. She offered up a silent prayer that Julia was right and it would not be a whip that was to be used on her. As the clock in the hall struck the hour, she knocked on the Correction Room door and entered, closing it behind her. She walked slowly across the room and knelt on the rug before the two seated men.

"Melanie," Craig's stern voice broke the ominous silence that had descended in the room. "By your own choice you are a slave. I have instructed you that it is the duty of a slave to show respect to all persons at all times. You not only broke that rule but you compounded your offence by doing so to a senior member of my family. Prepare yourself for punishment and present yourself to my father. Since your offence was committed against him, he will pronounce sentence."

Trying to stop shaking, Melanie rose, discarded the negligee and resumed her kneeling position facing Alex, a flush burning her face as she spread her knees wide and lowered her eyes to the floor.

"Julia has explained to you the meaning of 'Punishment Discipline' and why it is used. Do you fully understand it?" Alex asked, his voice sounding harsh in the silence.

"Yes, Sir," Melanie replied, unable to hide a slight tremble in her voice.

"Good," Alex continued. "You are to be put under 'Punishment Discipline' for the first five strokes of your punishment. In view of the seriousness of your offence, you are sentenced to fifteen strokes of this riding switch." He reached behind him and drew forth the implement named.

Melanie breathed an inward sigh of relief. Fifteen strokes was not as bad as she had envisaged, and even with the five penalty strokes, it would only be the same number of strokes as Craig had given her on her first beating, before she had asked for phase three. But she shuddered with terror as she raised her eyes and saw the switch. So that was what was in the parcel Alex had brought with him. It was longer than those Craig possessed, as long as the longest cane and was covered with plaited leather. A terrible thought flashed through her mind as she looked at it. 'It will cut me and make me bleed,' she thought.

"In view of the seriousness of your offence," Craig's voice broke into her thoughts. "I consider that a sound lesson across your back and buttocks with the whip is called for. However, my father says he is, for this time, content that the punishment be applied with the switch. Whilst I reluctantly concur with his wishes, I amend your sentence. You will be placed under 'Double Punishment Discipline' for the first six strokes. Position yourself for punishment," Craig ordered.

Melanie shuddered as she heard his words. She knew she could not take five, let alone six strokes in silence. So instead of twenty she would get twenty seven strokes. She remained static after Craig's pronouncement, other than to raise her eyes to him.

"Your slave requests permission to speak, please Master?" Her eyes, and the tremor in her voice, betrayed the terror that she was feeling.

"Permission granted," Craig replied.

Melanie turned her head and looked at Alex's expressionless face. "Sir," she began the speech that she had dreaded making. "I am guilty of a very serious offence against you. To ensure that you are completely satisfied that my lesson is properly learned, I humbly beg that you will be the one who administers my punishment and that you do so without mercy."

Alex looked at Craig, who nodded his agreement.

"Certainly," he said, looking down at Melanie. "It will be a pleasure." It was the truth. He would enjoy beating his daughter-in-law's luscious bottom.

"I submit myself to your pleasure, Sir," Melanie said.

She rose, turned, and walked to the wooden post. She took a deep breath and bent over the bar, feeling the short plank press against her stomach. She rested her shoulders on the forward bar and stretched her arms along its length. She gripped the bar tight. She remained still as Julia secured her wrist and ankle cuffs, secured her upper arms to the bar with the leather straps and then took up her position, kneeling in front of the bound girl. The silence in the room was broken as Alex rose and taking off his jacket, took up his position to the left of the bent girl.

"Remember, stay silent and good luck," Julia whispered, reaching forward and laying her hand on Melanie's arm.

Melanie felt Julia suddenly grip her arm tight. The signal! Heard the hiss as the switch sped through the air and the loud sharp report as it lashed across her taut bottom.

Crack.

Melanie's head jerked up and Julia saw the look of utter disbelief spread across her face at the sheer force of the stroke. Of all the beatings she had taken, Melanie had never felt a first stroke hurt so much. Her buttocks clenched and unclenched spasmodically in an effort to ease the agony that had erupted in her cheeks. She had only just managed to stifle the cry that rose in her throat. She still had to take five more and keep silent. That she must do at all costs, for failure to do so would mean she would have to take the twelve extra strokes, and that would be more than she could endure. She heard Julia call out, 'One!'.

Thwack.

Again the pressure on her arm was followed instantly by another report and another line of flaming pain in her bottom. As she struggled in her bonds, she felt a fine sweat dampen her skin as tears flowed from her eyes. Julia certainly was right, Alex did lay it on harder than his son! She tried to banish from her mind that there were at least thirteen more strokes to come.

"Two!" Julia's voice called the count.

Crack.

Even the warning pressure of Julia's hand did not help as the switch laced across her cheeks for the third time. The agony searing in her bottom was almost breaching her pain threshold. A terrible scream welled up in her throat and it required all her control to hold it back. She raised her eyes and looked through her tears at Julia, seeking some assistance to see her through the next three strokes.

"Three!" Julia called out, then added in a whisper that

only Melanie could hear. "Hold on! Only three more to come then you can scream as much as you like."

Thwack.

Melanie writhed and struggled against her bonds as the fourth line of fire burst across her bottom. She raised her head towards Julia, and her friend saw the look of defeat in her eyes. Melanie's head drooped and her body relaxed over the frame.

"Four!" Julia called out, then whispered. "Hold on! You can make it!" She prayed silently, anxious for Melanie to survive the first part of her ordeal.

Crack.

Melanie's head jerked up. Her mouth opened, her lips drawn back over her teeth, in a silent scream.

"Five!" Julia called out, and willed Alex to lay on the next stroke as quickly as possible.

But it did not come quick enough for Melanie. As her body relaxed as the switch fell away, the mounting pain in her bottom broke her control.

"Aaaarrrggggghhh!" A long drawn out scream echoed the report of the stroke in the silent room. Melanie lay writhing and struggling over the frame as loud sobs followed the scream. She knew she had failed and she must endure the extra strokes.

Craig had watched closely, leaning forward in his seat, as his father had laid on the first four strokes. Each had raised a livid red weal on Melanie's pale buttocks. His father was not holding back and each stroke whistled through the air sinking into Melanie's cheeks before dropping away leaving behind a burning weal. He had been very impressed by the way his slave had endured the four strokes and had secretly hoped she would remain silent until the seventh landed. Her scream on the fifth came as a great disappointment to him. His slave had let him down, and he determined that she would pay for doing so.

71

Before Alex could deliver the sixth stroke, Craig called to him to wait. He rose and approached the frame. He pulled a long strap tightly over his slave's waist, securing her to the short plank, saying to his father that it would prevent her wriggling too much and spoiling his aim. Before he resumed his seat, he looked at Melanie's bottom. Tightening the strap round her waist had forced her bottom upwards, tautening her cheeks. He grinned his satisfaction and, nodding to his father to continue, regained his seat.

Thwack.

"Aaaaaarrrgghhh! Noooooo!" Melanie screamed louder as a terrible pain erupted in her bottom. Despite the bonds on her ankles, the force of the stroke had lifted her up onto her toes. She was trying to writhe frantically, her buttocks clenching and unclenching as wave after wave of agony seared in her cheeks.

Julia had ceased to count after Melanie had cried out. Now the only sound in the room was the impact of the switch on bare flesh and Melanie's screams and loud sobbing and mewing between each stroke. Julia had moved to stand behind Craig and cringed as she saw the seventh and eighth strokes leave bright red lines on Melanie's swollen cheeks. The suffering girl's body was drenched in sweat and she could see droplets falling from her pendant breasts to form pools on the floor with her tears.

The pain was so intense that Melanie had lost count. The terrible agony, its epicentre in her bottom, had now spread throughout her body. Through the pain, she realised that, as when Craig beat her, there was that usual sexual stimulation rising inside her. Now there was not only the pain to endure, she must ensure that she displayed no signs of her arousal!

Crack.

Thwack.

As the switch bit into the softer part of her bottom, just

above the join of her cheeks and thighs, Melanie's body jerked rigid against her bonds and her scream died away as she sank, collapsed, over the frame.

Julia, realising what had happened, rushed forward and held Alex's arm. "She's fainted," she said to him.

"Then get something to revive her," Alex ordered, unsympathetically. "She must be conscious for all of her punishment."

Julia hurried from the basement. She rushed up stairs to the kitchen and drew a bowl of cold water. She collected a bottle of smelling salts and a clean handkerchief that she carried in her handbag and quickly returned to the basement.

While Julia tended to the beaten girl, Alex sat down beside Craig and looked sideways at his son. To his surprise, Craig's face remained impassive as he looked at his slave's buttocks. They were badly swollen and several bright red lines testified where the switch had broken the skin. Secretly, Alex envied his son. There were times when Julia angered him so much that he wished he could beat her as hard as he was beating Melanie, but that was against the agreement they had made together. One day, he vowed, Julia would submit to him as a slave and then she would experience a real thrashing such as this.

At last Melanie returned to full consciousness, thanks to Julia's application of the cold cloth to her face and neck and the smelling salts under her nose.

"Is it over?" Melanie asked quietly as she saw Julia kneeling in front of her.

"I'm afraid not," Julia whispered back. "You have only had eight, so far. You still have nineteen strokes to come."

A deep groan issued from Melanie's throat at the news. She was not even half way through her ordeal. For the first time under punishment she had fainted, and she was ashamed. Somehow she must not do it again.

Thwack.

Crack.

Relentlessly, the switch continued to mete out her punishment. Struggling to hold on to her senses, Melanie writhed and screamed out loud as the furnace in her bottom was re-ignited. Waves of agony coursed through her body as she absorbed pain that she had never dreamed existed.

Thwack.

Crack.

Crack.

As Alex laid on those three strokes, Melanie screamed as each bit into her bottom. Again, she felt herself slip into unconsciousness as her body sought release from the pain.

Again, Alex waited until Julia had tended to the girl and brought her back to full consciousness, before lashing the switch across her flaming buttocks twice more to complete the first part of her sentence. Melanie screamed loudly as each bit into her bottom but, by some superhuman effort, she managed to hold on to a thread of consciousness.

Alex, breathing heavily from the exertion of the beating looked hard at Melanie's buttocks after delivering the fifteenth stroke. The weals made by the switch stood out proud. He stood to one side as Craig rose and went and stood in front of his slave. He reached down, grasped a handful of her hair and turned her face up towards his own.

"You failed to remain silent during the 'Discipline' period. I will now deliver the twelve penalty strokes for your disobedience," he said. He released Melanie's hair and her head sank down.

He took the switch from his father and took up position to the left of his slave. He raised the switch high over his shoulder. Twelve times it whistled through the air. Five loud screams echoed the report as Melanie's body writhed frantically over the frame, before collapsing over the bar. Only a jerk of her body, and an increase in the loudness of her moans, showed she was still conscious and aware as the last seven strokes added their measure of agony to her body. He put down the switch and resumed his seat beside his father. Julia stood, silent in sympathy with the punished girl, behind the men.

For a few minutes, Melanie's body jerked violently against her bonds, as if the switch was still lashing her buttocks. Then, as she fought to regain control, her body gradually ceased to writhe over the bar. A soft moaning and mewing issued from her open mouth as waves of pain flowed through her. She realised that she had survived her ordeal, although she was ashamed at having fainted twice during the beating. She was shattered at how hard Alex had beaten her, and she felt sincere sympathy for Julia who had to submit to him. The men surveyed her as she slowly came to. Her bottom was badly swollen and bruised. Dark purple bruise lines stood out from the hard raised ridges, from which rivulets of red mingled with her sweat to seep over her cheeks and down her thighs. When Craig deemed his slave had sufficiently recovered, he asked Julia to release her from the frame.

Melanie felt her bonds loosened, but stayed in position awaiting her master's order to rise. When it came, she eased her body upright, trying unsuccessfully to suppress the moan that rose in her throat. Fresh waves of pain shot through her buttocks as she turned and shuffled to where the men sat. Each step fuelled the pain in her bottom, and she nearly screamed out loud as she knelt and her heels sank into her bruises. She knelt there, her eyes demurely lowered with tears flowing freely from them, as sob after sob continued to rack her body. She was in such pain that she was not fully aware of her surroundings, only the intense burning in her bottom. The one thing that was clear in her mind was that she had saved herself the embarrassment of letting her arousal get beyond her control.

"I trust you have learned your lesson," Craig's voice cut through the silence, penetrating her befuddled mind, bringing her back to reality.

"Yes, Master," she replied, her voice trembling. She turned her head to look at Alex. "I apologise for my rudeness, Sir, and thank you for my punishment."

"Go and tidy yourself and continue with your duties," Craig commanded, dismissing her.

Melanie rose to her feet, turned, and walked slowly to the door. Once on the other side, her hands flew to her throbbing bottom. Her fingers gently felt over the network of hard raised weals, from which heat radiated. Although she had taken many more strokes before, it was still the worst thrashing she had ever endured and she prayed that she would never have to bend for a beating from Alex ever again. As she slowly climbed the stairs, she became aware of Julia following her.

"I've come to help you and soothe your poor bottom," Julia explained her presence.

"I'm not allowed to ease the pain until tomorrow," Melanie said. "If you do, and my Master finds out, I will be beaten again."

"It's alright," Julia placated her. "The men were so impressed by the way you endured the beating, they agreed that I may attend to you this time."

So saying, Julia led Melanie into the bathroom and while the beaten girl stood under the shower, she gently washed her body, removing the dried sweat and the lines of blood from her thighs and bottom. Julia gently patted her dry and led her into her bedroom and told her to lie, face down, on the bed. Taking a small jar from her pocket, Julia proceeded to lightly rub a soothing ointment over the suffering girl's bottom.

"You were right," Melanie whispered. "Alex certainly lays it on harder than Craig. I hope I never have to take another beating from him. It hurt like hell. I never thought I would ever be beaten until I lost consciousness. Thank you for using the cold cloth and smelling salts."

"You were very brave. I wish I were that brave when Alex punishes me. I hated having to bring you round but they were insistent that you felt every stroke," Julia said.

"I don't know how you survive," Melanie said, turning her head to look at her friend. "I would be tempted to run away if I thought I was to be beaten by him regularly."

"Fortunately, due to the conditions I insisted upon from the outset, he never has, or never will, thrash me as hard as he has just done you. But, even so, I do sometimes want to run away," Julia replied. "But I will let you into a secret. I hate the pain, it terrifies me, but being so completely dominated and at his mercy, turns me on."

Melanie was about to confess that Craig had the same effect on her, but decided to keep quiet, at least for the time being. Julia having finished attending to her, Melanie repaired her make up and tidied her hair and the two girls descended to the lounge, where the men awaited. Melanie presented her bottom to Craig and Alex for their inspection.

The subject of her beating, and the offence that brought it about, was not mentioned again. Melanie remained naked and continued with her duties until it was time for the guests to depart. As she held the door open for them, Alex turned to her.

"You're a brave girl, Melanie. I didn't expect you to take your punishment so well. Craig is a lucky fellow," he said, genuine approval showing on his face.

"Thank you, Sir," Melanie responded. Then an imp of mischief entered her mind as she added. "You certainly know how to beat a girl soundly. With respect, I hope you enjoyed disciplining me."

"I must confess I did. You have such a luscious bottom," he said, giving her a gentle pat on that part of her anatomy.

"I hope it is a pleasure you never have the opportunity to repeat. It hurt far too much!" Melanie answered coquettishly, failing to suppress a little giggle.

Goodbyes being finalised, Melanie closed the door behind the guests and followed Craig into the lounge. She sank to her knees before him.

"I trust you really have learned your lesson," he said, his eyes roving over her nakedness. "It was a very severe beating, but not more so than you deserved."

"I hope I have, Master," Melanie replied. "But it was not as bad as I had expected."

"Oh! And exactly what were you expecting?" Craig asked, a puzzled look on his face.

"I thought that in view of the seriousness with which you viewed my offence, I would get a severe lashing with one of the whips across my back, and probably also across my bottom. Knowing how strict you are on good manners," Melanie said, lowering her eyes. "I had prepared myself for a sound whipping."

"That is exactly what you deserved," Craig responded sternly. "Had I not decided to have my father thrash you, that is what would have happened. But the first time you feel the leather on your back, it will be me, and no other, that wields the whip."

"Yes, Master," Melanie replied demurely. "I would not want it any other way."

Craig retired to bed shortly after, ordering her to come to him. When she entered his room, Melanie saw that he was already lying on the bed, naked save for a sheet covering him. She slipped under the sheet and immediately he reached for her and turned her to her back. She spread her legs wide apart, feeling her arousal already tingling in her sex tunnel. He lost no time in entering her.

"You are forbidden to come," he ordered as he thrust deep into her.

The order took Melanie by surprise. He did not always give such an order and she had thought he would not torment her in that fashion after that terrible thrashing. She fought to hold back the orgasm that was already raging inside her. His taking was quick and fierce, causing her to writhe under him, her buttocks rubbing on the sheet reawakening the pain that still simmered there.

Such was the strength of Craig's arousal that it was not long before he shed his satisfaction deep into her. He fell to her side, leaving her feeling frustrated and unsatisfied. It was some minutes before he broke the silence.

"Did I notice that, while father beat you, you became aroused?"

"Yes, Master," Melanie stammered in reply. She was mortified that, despite all her efforts, she had let it be seen. She prayed that it was only Craig who had noticed. At least, if Alex or Jenny had noticed they had refrained from commenting.

"That is strange!" Craig mused. "I had hoped that it was only when I beat you that your body responded that way." It was no secret between them. After that first beating, Craig had let it be known that he did not disapprove and Melanie had not tried to hide it from him.

"I did try to conceal it this afternoon, Master," Melanie said softly, fearing that by not doing so she had displeased him. "As usual, I tried to concentrate on taking the punishment well, especially today to avoid breaking the rule of the Punishment Discipline. But your father hurt me so much that the fear of the extra strokes made me lose my concentration. I hope I have not displeased you, Master," She added the last hopefully.

Her words recalled to Craig's mind the picture of her naked body, bent over the bar, and the switch lashing into her soft bottom. She had writhed and screamed delightfully as Alex had laid the switch on with gusto. The image was so erotic that his manhood stiffened, again throbbing with his desire. He pulled her to him and mounted her. Such was the ferocity of his taking that, when he rescinded the earlier order, Melanie yelled her submission to him as her body was shattered by a series of orgasms that left her drained and in a state of semi-consciousness.

When she came to, he was fast asleep. She eased herself from the bed and retired to her own room.

CHAPTER 4.

After Craig had caned her that first time and he had informed her how a slave should behave, there had been the question of how she should dress when in the house. His answer had led to further questions that had firmly fixed in Melanie's mind her true status. His answers to those questions had filled her with trepidation and she had, in her innocence, thought that such occasions would not occur.

Now two of those answers had been proved to be correct. She had been beaten in front of witnesses and beaten by another man. She wondered how long it would be before the last answer would be put to the test. Fourteen months had now passed since the day of her submission. So far, that had been the one time that she had been beaten by anyone other than Craig and had been ordered to stay naked in front of him and Julia for the rest of the day. Alex had thrashed her so badly with the switch that she had made certain that she behaved herself impeccably in his presence. She certainly did not want a repeat of that encounter!

Since then, although visits to the Correction Room were not infrequent, there had been no other occasion. She had begun to believe that she would not be again beaten by anyone other than her master and that she would never be ordered to sexually serve anyone else. She was not aware of it, but her belief in the certainty that these things would never happen, meant she was living in a fool's paradise. The illusion was about to be shattered in the most unexpected, and unwelcome, manner as she embarked on the next stage of her journey.

As Craig's business increased, and expanded throughout the world, there was an increase in the number of visitors to his office. One of these was a Mr Yasimoto, a short stocky Japanese. Neither Melanie nor any of the other girls that worked in the office, could stand the man. Whilst his visits to the office were not often, his smarmy bearing, and the way he always seemed to be mentally undressing them, made them shudder with disgust. What made his visits even more unbearable was the way he always seemed to treat them as inferior beings.

One Wednesday Mr Yasimoto called at the office. Melanie squirmed inwardly as he closed the door and turned his penetrating gaze on her, the lecherous, ever present gleam in his eyes. She rose and entered Craig's office, mindful of how his small eyes would have been fastened on her bottom as she walked away from him. Angry at the way he had ogled her, she forgot herself.

"That leering Jap is here, Sir," she said. She always called her Master 'Sir' in the office, even when they were alone, as he had ordered. What she was unaware of was that the man in question had followed her and heard her every word.

Craig's face turned red with anger as he rose and welcomed the visitor, at the same time apologising for her rudeness. The rest of the day passed without incident until the other girls had gone home and Melanie was left alone with her Master. As she expected, he summoned her into his office. She stood facing his desk awaiting the explosion she had dreaded all day. It did not come. Instead, in a level voice devoid of emotion, he gave her an order. At first she didn't believe that he was serious and nearly burst out laughing. Surely he wouldn't beat her in front of the man all the office staff despised? Then she saw the anger in his eyes and knew that he was deadly serious and that she had no choice but to do as he commanded.

As a consequence, she spent a very embarrassing half-hour in the hotel where the Japanese was staying. Even more embarrassing than when she had been sent on the same errand to Alex's office. When she left, she had again explained, in detail, her relationship with Craig and the methods he used to punish her, and begged the man to witness the punishment she would receive for her outburst. Since her offence had been committed against him, Craig had offered him the chance to decide on what her punishment should be. What troubled her most was that Craig's invitation was for the man to come to the house on Saturday morning and stay over night until he was due to go to the airport and fly back home on the Sunday morning. What had disturbed her more than anything else had been the undisguised gleam of pure lechery, and pleasure, that had been on his face as she had explained her status and begged him to accept the invitation. The look had been even more disconcerting when she explained that she would be naked, both for the beating and afterwards.

Melanie rose early on Saturday morning with an intense feeling of dread, organised Craig's breakfast and ensured that the house was ready to receive the visitor. Then she went upstairs to prepare herself in accordance with her master's instructions. She showered, making sure her hair did not get wet. As she looked at her reflection in the mirror, she was relieved to see that the evidence of her last beating had disappeared. Her buttocks had reverted to their natural pale softness, a matter that would shortly be altered. She applied her make up and perfume carefully and brushed her hair until it hung in a shiny cascade down her back. Then she put on a very revealing white negligee. Craig had made no concessions. She went downstairs and waited in a blind panic for the guest to arrive.

Mr Yasimoto arrived punctually, by taxi, at eleven. Melanie tried hard to hide her embarrassment at his lascivious gaze roamed over her near naked body as she answered his knock on the door. He did not bother to conceal his admiration of the body the negligee failed to cover up. He put down his suitcase, but retained his hold on a long thin parcel. She ushered him into the lounge where Craig waited and then took his case up to the room she had prepared for him. She served coffee in the lounge and left the men to talk as she went to put the final touches to lunch. She served lunch in the dining room, trying to keep her hands from shaking as she placed plates before the men and poured wine into their glasses. She listened carefully to their chat, hoping to get some idea of what was in store for her, but no mention was made either of her offence or the punishment to come. No wiser, she finally cleared the table and served coffee in the lounge. As she left the lounge, Craig called after her and ordered her to report to the Correction Room at three o'clock.

She waited in growing trepidation for the time of her ordeal to come. Having had Jenny witness her being beaten, when Alex had switched her so badly, she had expected not to feel so self conscious about anyone else seeing her punished. In fact, she had thought that such a display of her submissiveness was, in a way, exciting. But this was to be in front of the hated Mr Yasimoto! She shook with fear and embarrassment as she descended the stairs and, as the clock in the hall struck three, she knocked on the Correction Room door and entered. She walked slowly across the room and sank to her knees before the seated men. A heavy silence filled the room as she kept her eyes lowered.

"Melanie." Craig's voice broke the silence. "You have greatly insulted Mr Yasimoto. I will not tolerate such behaviour from you. You have been summoned here for punishment. To ensure that you have taken no steps to reduce the effect of the lesson you are about to receive, you will present yourself to Mr Yasimoto to be tested."

This was an addition to the normal routine and one which Craig had explained to her earlier. She rose, fetched a long feather from its place on the side table and handed it to the Japanese. She stood with her back to him, untied the sash on the negligee and let it slide down, exposing her back and buttocks. She remained perfectly still and concentrated. Very lightly, he touched her back, buttocks and thighs in several places with the tip of the feather. She nearly moved in terror as the feather touched her back the first time. Did this mean that she was to be whipped? And for the first time in front of the him of all people? But, as soon as she felt the touch, she called out 'Now'.

When the Japanese informed Craig that he was satisfied, she adjusted the negligee and returned to her kneeling position. She waited with bated breath to hear what her fate was to be. Since it was both her back and buttocks that had been tested, she was sure that Craig, contrary to what he had always maintained, intended to use a whip on her back for the first time. She felt angry both at this betrayal, as she thought of it, and the fact that her Master had not taken a whip to her before. It was something she had wished he would do for some time now.

"Mr Yasimoto is satisfied with the test," Craig announced. "Prepare."

Trying to hide her disgust, and shame, at having to bare herself in front of the Japanese, Melanie removed the negligee, casting it to one side, and spread her knees wide. She felt her face flush as she imagined the guest staring at her exposed sex.

"You are guilty of extreme rudeness to my client here," Craig began to announce her sentence. "You are to be thrashed across your backside. Twenty-four strokes with the implement of Mr Yasimoto's choice."

Melanie had raised her eyes to hear her sentence. She continued to watch with mounting fear, as the Japanese reached behind his chair and drew forth the long thin package he had brought with him. He began to unwrap it. As the last wrapping was removed, Melanie stared in dreadful fascination at what was revealed. She saw a long thick rattan cane. One end had been split down for eighteen inches into four equal sized strips. She nearly cried out in alarm as she saw that the edges of the split ends were razor sharp. It was going to be agony!

"This is what is used on displeasing women in my country," Mr Yasimoto said gravely. "Especially when they need a lesson in respect. It is usually very effective." He added, looking at Craig. "After your kind invitation, I had it sent over by special courier."

"That was very thoughtful," Craig acknowledged. Then he looked down on Melanie. "Position!" he ordered sharply.

Melanie hesitated for a second. She had thought of trying to please her Master by asking the guest to beat her. Then she remembered the force that Alex had used on her. The Japanese looked very muscular, despite his short stature, and her courage deserted her, especially as she was sure that even moderately hard strokes of that dreadful cane would cut her badly. She rose, bowed to Mr Yasimoto, and walked to the bars. Taking a deep breath, she positioned her ankles for binding and bent forward reaching to the longer bar, along which she stretched her arms and gripped tight with her small hands.

She felt Craig secure her ankles and then her wrists. Then, to her horror, he fitted the wide strap across her waist and pulled it tight, locking her against the plank. She tried to wriggle her behind, but she was held perfectly immobile. She sensed Craig picking up the cane and tasking his position. Her breathing quickened in anticipation of the flogging to come as he lightly laid the cane against her quivering cheeks to measure his distance.

Thwack.

Melanie sucked in her breath through her clenched teeth as a sudden fire erupted in her bottom.

Crack.

A second sheet of fire joined the first. She could feel the

split ends of the cane spreading on impact so that a wider area was covered by each stroke.

Thwack.

"Arrrrrgggggggh!" A cry of pain and despair followed the report. She tried to wriggle to ease the pain, but was too securely held. Only three strokes taken and she had another twenty-one to come, she shuddered as she thought of the damage the split cane would do to her bottom.

Accustomed as she was to being beaten, she knew, even at this early stage in the proceedings, that this dreadful cane would break her control earlier than usual. Each time the cane struck, it was like receiving four strokes at once! But, under no circumstances, must she beg for mercy. Rather let Yasimoto see her become aroused than disgrace herself in that manner!

Thwack.

Crack.

Melanie yelled, loud and long, as each stroke bit into her taut bottom. Her eyes shed tears that dropped to the floor, and she felt a light sweat break out over her skin.

Thwack.

Crack.

Thwack

The fire in her bottom had now become a furnace, as Craig laid these strokes on in quick succession. Whether he thought she deserved no mercy or he was trying to impress his guest, she did not know, but he was certainly laying the strokes on with terrible force.

Thwack.

Crack.

The first full-bloodied screams followed these two strokes as the pain broke her control. She tried to writhe in her bonds, to no avail. She had been concentrating on trying to keep count and breathed a sigh of relief as she realised she had reached the half-way mark of her ordeal.

Craig stood back to regain his breath. He was deliberately laying the cane across her rear with all his force. He was determined that she would be taught a sound lesson in respect. One that she would not forget in a hurry! He looked at her backside to check the state it was in. Her buttocks were no longer milky white. Now they were literally covered by a mass of dark red lines which stretched the full width of her cheeks, curling round both sides. The split ends of the cane had made many of the weals overlap, and already some of the raised ridged weals were weeping bright red where the sharp edges of had cut into her skin. He felt no compassion for his slave. She had disgraced both herself and him and fully deserved all that she was suffering.

He returned to his position, ready to deliver the other half of her punishment. He raised his arm high over his shoulder.

Thwack.

Crack.

Melanie's screams echoed round the room and, as they died away, a deep groan followed as she became aware, through the pain, that the arousal in her belly was getting out of control. She knew she still had many more strokes to come before her punishment was complete. At that moment, she would have given anything to be spared the agony that they would add to the furnace raging in her bottom. A furnace that had now spread throughout her entire body! The presence of the Japanese, which had troubled her initially, was now forgotten. Her world had shrunk to be concentrated on her buttocks and her belly.

Crack.

Melanie's head jerked up as the split end of the cane lashed into the soft under side of her buttocks. Her lips drew back over her teeth in a silent scream. Her body arched back, her limbs straining against her bonds until she suddenly collapsed over the frame. She had not felt such pain before, not even when Alex had beaten her, but she knew that she must endure it to the end. There was no escape!

Thwack.

Crack.

Two more rapid strokes lashed where the last one had struck. Melanie's head shook violently from side to side, sending a cascade of sweat and tears arcing across the room, forming a rainbow in the bright light.

Craig lashed the last five strokes of her punishment across his slave's buttocks. More raised ridges appeared almost instantly, glowing bright red where more cuts opened, yet there was hardly any reaction from the bent girl. Only a jerk as each landed and an even louder moan testified that she was feeling the extra pain being inflicted. He replaced the cane, released Melanie's bonds and resumed his seat beside his guest.

Mr Yasimoto had sat silent, watching closely as the thrashing was administered, his face impassive. Secretly, he was impressed by this English girl's fortitude. When he and Craig had decided on her punishment, he had thought that she would not last even to the half way mark before screaming for mercy. He had prided himself that only one of his own countrywomen could endure a punishment of that severity. He had been mistaken! It had also come as a culture shock to him that corporal punishment was practised in a European household and also the fact that the girl acted as, and was treated as, a slave was something he had certainly not expected to find.

Melanie was hardly aware of the last five strokes searing their path across her swollen and blazing bottom. A jerk, a shower of sweat and an animal like mewing was her only reaction to each impact. The pain had reached the limit of her endurance and she had sunk into a hazy cocoon of mist, her only conscious thought being that she must, under no circumstances, beg for mercy. A few minutes after Craig had released her bonds she slowly began to emerge from the fog of agony into which she had sunk. Summoning up all her control, she eased her pain racked body upright from the bars. Keeping her hands away from her bottom, she turned and shuffled to where the men sat. As she sank to her knees, spreading them wide, a stifled cry escaped her lips as her heels sank into her throbbing cheeks. She kept her eyes lowered, too ashamed to look up and see the cruel lustful look that she knew would be present on the guest's face.

"Your punishment and offence will be entered in your record book," Craig told her. "Together with this warning. Should you commit a similar offence at any time in the future, your back will feel the teaching of a whip. Now, go and clean yourself and continue with your duties."

"Yes Master," Melanie replied through the sobs that still racked her body. "I thank my Master for my beating." She completed the usual ritual and forced herself to raise her eyes to the Japanese. "I am sorry for having offended you and beg your forgiveness."

"The matter is closed," Mr Yasimoto replied, keeping any hint of emotion from his voice.

Trying to favour her throbbing bottom as much as possible, Melanie rose and left the room. She made her way gingerly upstairs to the bathroom. She cleaned herself under a shower, removing the evidence of her arousal from her thighs. When she went to her bedroom, she dared to look at her bottom in the mirror. A gasp of horror escaped her mouth at the sight that met her eyes. Gone was the clear white smoothness that she spent hours nurturing for Craig's pleasure. A mass of hard ridges covered the whole surface of her cheeks, the few areas between being coloured by the purple of severe bruising. She shuddered at the many places where the skin had been broken by the sharp edges of the cane. Her behind looked far worse than it had done when Alex had beaten her!

A feeling of pride swept through her, though. She had stoically endured yet another terrible beating without bringing disgrace down on her Master. She turned from the frightening sight and commenced to repair her appearance. Fifteen minutes after leaving the Correction Room, she entered the lounge and stood before the men for their inspection. The only visible signs that remained of her ordeal were the bruises on her bottom and the redness in her eyes from the weeping.

Trying to overcome her embarrassment and hide the humiliation and her dislike for the intruder in her life from showing on her face, she continued with her duties for the remainder of the day. No mention was made of her offence, or her punishment, although she was aware that Mr Yasimoto took every opportunity to stare at her naked body, especially her bottom. She waited impatiently for bedtime to come, hoping that Craig would order her to his bed.

She breathed a sigh of relief when their guest finally retired to his room. She was about to go upstairs herself, when Craig called her back into the lounge.

"Mr Yasimoto, in case you are not already aware is to return home tomorrow. There he has agreed to negotiate a very lucrative contract for my business. I want to be certain that he is more than delighted with his stay here." Craig looked hard at her and Melanie trembled as she sensed what he was about to say. "He is very taken with you, not only with your looks but also the excellent way you took your punishment. You will go to your room and make yourself beautiful. You will then go to his room and place yourself at his disposal for the night."

Melanie stared at him in horror as he put her worst fears into words. A feeling of nausea swept through her and she was nearly physically sick on the spot. She had always been aware that it was inevitable that the time would come when she would be ordered to please another man. But to have to lie with that gross creature upstairs! It was too much and she was on the verge of rebelling against Craig for the first time.

"You will please him in whatever way he requires. Should I receive a bad report from him in the morning, you will be put over the bars and I will let him loose on you with that cane he gave me."

Melanie stared at him in disbelief as his words sank in, and her face turned white with shock. She knew Craig did not make idle threats. The very idea of bending over the bars, naked, while Yasimoto gloated as he thrashed her unmercifully, as she knew he would, was more than she could bear. Rather go to his bed than that! She lowered her head in capitulation.

"If that is your order, Master," she stammered. "I will obey and do my best to please him."

With her master's threat foremost in her mind, Melanie made her way upstairs to her room. She quickly checked her appearance and added more perfume. She took a final look in the mirror and, being satisfied, made her way to the guest's room. Resigning herself to whatever trial might await her, she knocked on the door.

"Enter."

She passed through the doorway, closed the door behind her, and dropped to her knees.

"My Master has ordered me to present myself to you, Sir," she said softly. "I am to serve your pleasure in any way you wish."

A lecherous smile spread across his face. He beckoned her to him and indicated that she should kneel in front of him. Melanie shuffled forward on her knees until her face was a few inches away from the silk kimono that he had put on. He untied the sash and let the garment fall apart. He was quite naked beneath it, obviously he had expected her attendance. Melanie felt the bile rose in her throat as she saw his fat, flabby, stomach only inches in front of her face. She lowered her eyes and saw his half flaccid penis, which dangled above a wrinkled sac, protruding from a mass of jet black hair.

With her master's threat still fresh in her mind, Melanie swallowed her revulsion, leaned forward and placed her lips on the end of the shaft. She began to kiss and lick it lightly. She heard a sigh above her as the object of her attentions began to harden and grow. She closed her mouth over the crown, feeling it start to throb as his desire began to rise. She sensed the garment slide from his shoulders as he reached down and grasped the back of her neck. He forced her head forward, until his cock reached deep into her throat, nearly making her throw up. She managed to control the impulse and continued to suck and lick him.

Just as she thought she was going to choke, he pulled back, withdrawing his manhood. He grasped a handful of her hair and hoisted her to her feet. Tears sprang to her eyes. Showing unexpected strength, he picked her up and carried her to the bed, on which he deposited her unceremoniously. As he descended on her, Melanie spread her thighs wide. Without any preliminaries, he thrust his shaft into her body. Despite her revulsion, his entry, and the feel of his penis thrusting in her vagina, she felt herself become aroused. She closed her eyes and concentrated her mind on containing her reaction. The last thing she wanted him to believe was that she was deriving pleasure from his usage.

"You are forbidden to come," he ordered as his mouth, with its sweet smelling breath, descended on hers.

The man's virility astounded her. No sooner had he shed his desire into her tunnel, rolled off her and caught his breath, than he was on her again. Several times he used her, each taking being as savage as the first. At last, to Melanie's relief, he slid off her and appeared to fall asleep. She waited, to make sure, before leaving the room. As she looked at him, she remembered that he had watched her flogged, had even provided that terrible cane that had been used on her and she recalled the sadistic smile that had edged his mouth as he had unwrapped it before her eyes. Now he had used her savagely, denying her the release he must have known her body craved, and left her with a deep sense of frustration. She resolved that she would not let him get away with treating her in such a cavalier manner.

Deciding to risk his displeasure, and the inevitable whipping that would surely follow, she knelt astride the unconscious form. She began to stroke the inside of his thighs lightly with her fingertips. Moving slowly up towards his sac, she smiled to herself as she saw his penis start to engorge as she reawakened his desires. She changed her position until the crown of his organ was brushing her sex lips. Her own arousal surged. She judged the moment perfectly. As his eyes opened in astonishment, she thrust down on his now rigid shaft and began to fuck him as hard as she could. His head lifted up, surprise and anger on his face at her audacity. He opened his mouth but, before he could utter a word, she leaned over and crushed her mouth hard against his, her tongue forcing a path between his teeth.

She increased her momentum, even more so when his hands suddenly clasped her buttocks in a fierce grip, renewing the pain of her thrashing that still simmered there. To her dismay, he forced her mouth away from his and clamped his teeth around one of her hard nipples. As his teeth closed on her teat, sending sharp pains soaring through it, she fucked him as hard as she could, her internal muscles tightening on his stalk milking it for all she was worth. As he writhed and panted under her, Melanie suddenly realised that, for once she was in control. Savouring her revenge, she slowed down her efforts before he could climax. She proceeded to tease him, bringing him close to the point of ejection and then slackening off, time and time again. The expression on his face, and in his eyes, was a joy for her to behold, one minute savage desire, the next wild anger.

Finally, aware that she could not hold his ejection, or her own arousal, in check any longer, she plunged frantically up and down until, with cries of fulfilment, they both came. Melanie's inside continued to milk him to the last drop before she surrendered to the darkness brought on by the shattering orgasms that raged through her body. It was sometime later that Melanie regained consciousness and rolled off his body. She realised that, this time, he had succumbed to exhaustion and was sound asleep. She crept from the chamber and returned to her own room.

She awoke on time the next morning, washed and put on her make up and brushed out her hair. Her buttocks still hurt from the thrashing and her sex lips and tunnel felt bruised from the savage way she had fucked him. Normally, the morning after a beating she was allowed to wear her negligee. But this morning, she decided to remain naked and torment the Japanese. If she was to be whipped for her disobedience and audacity the night before, she would make it worth while! She served her master, and his guest, their morning tea and ran their baths.

Throughout breakfast, and all through the morning, she expected to be summoned to the Correction Room to atone for her sins. The satisfaction she secretly enjoyed at the memory of her revenge would make any whipping, or even another dose of that split cane in the hands of the Japanese, would be worth while. To her surprise, nothing was said. Even when Craig returned from taking his guest to the airport, no mention was made of her offence. Melanie mentally chalked this up as a major triumph, one that she would savour for a long time to come.

The daily routine continued. Melanie, fearing another beating before her buttocks had recovered from that caning, did her best to avoid displeasing her Master. She was relieved when Craig did not even summon her to the Correction Room for his pleasure.

CHAPTER 5.

Several weeks passed and still no mention was made of Melanie's disobedience or her treatment of the Japanese. Once her buttocks had recovered, she was still summoned to the Correction Room at intervals but this was to atone for different offences, or for her Master's pleasure. So far, Melanie thought to herself one morning, she had been beaten by Alex with Jenny watching, beaten in front of the Japanese and made to submit herself to the pleasures of that man. Secretly she regarded these as tests of her submission set by her Master, and, if Craig's comments were of note, she had passed on all counts. She wondered what further trials he would set for her before he was finally convinced of her total submission.

She had been his slave for a year now and, to her consternation, he had still not used a whip on her. Why was this, she wondered? As much as she feared a whipping on her back, or any other part of her tender body, she regarded this as one step towards her complete slavery that she wanted to take. She had seen the whips hanging on the Correction Room wall many times and often wondered what it would be like to be put under one. In the privacy of her bed, she had tried to visualise her naked body tied to the whipping post as the lash curled round her soft body. In her mind, she heard her screams and watched her body writhe in pain. Just thinking about it made her juices flow and her needs burn within her, so much so that she just had to caress herself into an orgasm to relieve the urges that ravaged within her.

She was aware that Craig had been engaging in some correspondence, the nature of which he kept from her. Melanie did not like to be kept in the dark and, as the weeks passed, she became increasingly concerned that something was afoot. Something that she would not like and that would test her even further. Fear of the unknown was always worse, she tried to tell herself, than the actual event! She was going about her duties one Wednesday evening, when Craig summoned her to his study. He indicated that she should sit on the chair facing his desk.

"I have been intrigued by some advertisements in one of the magazines I have acquired," Craig said, looking at a small pile of them in front of him.

Melanie craned her neck forward to see what they could be about and her blood ran cold. The covers of two were visible and each portrayed an S & M scene. She looked at Craig, puzzled as to how these could concern her. A terrible idea sprang to her mind. Surely he was not going to make her pose for pictures in them, probably with marks, and not artificial ones at that, clearly etched on her body!

"Apparently there are several groups of people, with similar relationships and tastes, to ours, who meet on occasions for a couple of days. I have been in contact with one of these and we have been invited to attend their next weekend meeting which will be next Saturday. We are to arrive early in the morning and leave again sometime after lunch on the Sunday," Craig explained. "On the Saturday morning, the men draw lots to see which of the girls will serve them for the remainder of the time."

Melanie felt terror grip her as she listened to the last sentence. So this was to be another test of her submission! She was to serve some total stranger while her own master enjoyed the pleasure of an equally unknown woman. It was as if she had fallen asleep and was in the midst of a terrible nightmare. She looked up at Craig, who had stopped talking, obviously waiting for her to say something.

"Does that mean that, whoever draws me, will beat me? Will I be beaten badly?" she asked, hesitantly, although she knew in her mind what the answer would be.

"Yes," Craig replied. "On the Saturday morning, each girl is required to submit to a thrashing from her temporary Master, to demonstrate her willingness to serve him for the weekend. The implement to be used, and the number of strokes, is determined by a secret draw beforehand." He paused to let this sink in before adding. "It is only the girls' bottoms that may be beaten and no whips are allowed."

Melanie remained silent. So this was why she had not been summoned to the Correction Room for two weeks. To ensure that her body was unmarked, was a clean slate for her unknown tormentor to decorate.

Again she hesitated before asking another question. "Will I have to submit to this man sexually?" A silly question, whose answer she could already devise!

"Naturally!" Craig answered. "He will have total rights over your body and you must submit in any way he may require. Although I have been told it has never happened yet, if any man is seriously dissatisfied with a girl's performance, he reports the matter to the gathering on the Sunday after breakfast. The girl is then whipped across her back, usually by her true Master, in front of all present."

Melanie shuddered. So far, Craig had still not used a whip on any part of her body, much to her disappointment, and, when this did happen for the first time she wanted it to be in the privacy of his Correction Room. Not with others watching. With that threat hanging over them, she could believe that no girl would let herself be found wanting.

"There is one other thing," Craig continued. "All the girls, on arrival, have to change into a certain type of costume. We will have to call on the theatrical costumier in town tomorrow and select one for you. I think that is all for now, you may continue with whatever you were doing."

Melanie rose and left the room to do as he had ordered. She fretted for the rest of that day and the next morning until lunchtime. Craig called her to his office and told her to go with him. They got into his car, drove to another part of the town and parked outside a small warehouse. They entered and were met by an effeminate man who asked what he could do for them.

"My young lady is attending a fancy dress party and needs a costume. One similar to that worn by an Eastern dancing girl in the films," Craig informed him.

There followed several embarrassing minutes for Melanie as the man produced several costumes for Craig to choose from. He finally decided on two and the purchase was completed. When they arrived home that evening, the first thing Craig did was to order her to change into each for him to select the one she would wear. Melanie modelled them for him. They were similar in design, each comprising a transparent skirt that hung, suspended from a jewelled and spangled belt that fastened by a clasp to one side of her hips, and a face veil that clipped to her ears. Both skirts consisted of two chiffon panels, one much narrower than the other which hung down her front. One had a tiny bolero jacket, which did not meet in front and exposed her full firm breasts, the other consisted of two round almost conical cups to cover her breasts, with a front fastening, and which were held in place by fine chains round her back and neck. Both costumes had a pair of knickers, but Craig was adamant that she would not be allowed to wear these under the skirt. After a lot of thought, he made his choice.

"On Friday, you will pack a case with this costume and your toilet necessities," he ordered. "Nothing else!"

They left the house early on the Saturday, Craig driving his car, and set out for the venue where the meeting would take place. Melanie was in a state of nervousness. What she had been told so far had filled her with dread. Her apprehension was not allayed when, after driving for an hour, Craig pulled in to a lay-by. He placed a blindfold over her eyes, explaining the girls were not allowed to see the neighbourhood, or the outside of the house they were going to. She sat there as he drove off, unable to see and her feeling of dread increasing with every minute.

The car eventually stopped. She heard Craig get out and then the door at her side opened. He assisted her out and led her across a gravel surface and up some steps. A doorbell rang, the door opened and they were greeted by a deep male voice. She heard the door close behind her and the cover was removed from over her eyes. She blinked in the sunlight that streamed through the windows and looked round. She was in a large oak panelled hall, off which several doors led, with a wide staircase leading to a horse-shoe shaped landing.

"You must be Melanie." The deep voice brought her back to reality. "I'm Paul. This is my house and, for the purposes of this weekend, I am the Senior Master." He clapped his hands and a door at the far end of the hall opened and a beautiful woman, who Melanie guessed to be about thirty years old, glided across the parquet floor. "This is my wife, Yasmin, who will supervise the girls." He turned to Melanie. "You will go with her and, as this is your first time, she will show you the ropes."

"Come with me, Melanie, and I'll show you to your room and explain the rules and procedures." Yasmin's voice was soft and husky and betrayed a slight accent, which Melanie could not place, although the woman's face did look slightly Middle-Eastern.

Yasmin led her up the stairs and stopped by a small table on which there were several plain envelopes.

"Choose an envelope and once you're alone in your room, take out the piece of paper. It will have on it your identification number, by which you will be summoned to the Dungeon. You will destroy the paper and tell no one, except your natural Master, what the number is," Yasmin told her.

Melanie picked up an envelope.

Yasmin led her to a room and led her in. It was lovely, light and airy, with sunlight shining through the window. There was a side room in which there was a bath, shower, wash basin and toilet. Melanie felt a slight shudder pass over her as she saw the large double bed, already made up, which had metal frames at its head and foot, to which chains were attached at each corner post.

"This will be your room," Yasmin repeated. "You must change into your costume, now, and attend to your make up. You are the first to arrive so will wait here until the other girls have settled in and I will come and get you and we will all go down together."

Resigning herself to the inevitable, Melanie unpacked the suitcase and changed as ordered. Yasmin watched her closely, inspected the final result her and told her to sit on one of the chairs.

"You are very beautiful," Yasmin said with total sincerity. Then she went on to explain the rules by which the girls must abide and the procedures that governed the weekend. When she had finished, she asked if there were any questions. Receiving none, she rose to leave the room.

"I must go and welcome the other girls. You must wait here until I come for you," she said. "In case Craig has not already told you, there are only six of us this weekend."

Melanie opened the envelope and extracted the piece of paper. On it was written the number '4'. She flushed the paper down the toilet and sat down on a chair, her mind going over all that she had been told. Secretly she cursed Craig for bringing her there. The next eighteen hours or so would be a trial, terrifyingly so because, although things had been explained in detail, there was still an element of the unknown to face. She heard other female voices on the landing, the opening and shutting of doors and then silence fell. An ominous silence that seemed to go on for ages!

Then the sound of doors opening came to her ears. Her door opened and Yasmin beckoned her out. Melanie emerged on to the landing to find that Yasmin had discarded her long housecoat, to display a perfect figure clad in a harem costume similar in design to her own. Four other girls, all very beautiful and similarly attired, were standing there and Yasmin introduced them as, Nicola, Jenny, Judy and Annette.

Yasmin led the girls down to the kitchen where they prepared coffee, which they served to the six men in the lounge. Whilst serving Craig, Melanie whispered her number to him. As the men drank their coffee and smoked, Melanie looked round at the other men. It was not necessary for her to know their names, as all the girls must only address them as 'Master'. They all looked to be around the thirty to forty age group and were quite handsome. Melanie felt a slight stirring in her belly as she wondered which she would be partnered with. One, however, caught her eye more than the others. He had a pale olive skin and his eyes were very dark and forbidding, and there was a cruel curl to his mouth as he surveyed the girls. She heard Paul call him 'Hassan'. When coffee was over, and the crockery cleared away, the men and girls were assembled in the lounge

"Quiet everyone." Paul's voice silenced the room. "It is now time for the draw to take place and the acts of submission to be performed." He held up seven sealed white envelopes. "For the benefit of our newest members, I will explain how the pairings, and submission, are decided." He pointed to three piles of envelopes, white, red green. He picked up the white pile. "There is a card inside each envelope. Three cards for the cane, two for the tawse and one each for the birch and riding switch, the implements to be used today." He laid the envelopes on a side table. He indicated two other piles of envelopes already on the table. "Each pile contains playing cards from the eight upwards." He said. "Court cards count as eleven, twelve and thirteen respectively, The face value of the cards indicates the number of strokes." He fanned the red and green cards out on the table.

He looked round and ordered the girls to kneel in a row along one side of the room. "First the men will choose their slave." He fanned out six further cards in his hand, each bore a number from one to six clearly on view, and offered them around. One by one the men took a card. Melanie found out later that the men were forbidden to take their own slave's number.

"Now the slaves will make their choice so see how they are to demonstrate their submission." He looked at the line of kneeling girls. "Nicola first."

Nicola rose and approached the table. With nervous fingers she selected one white, one red and one green envelope and placed them in a larger fourth envelope, which she sealed. Then, so that not even Paul could see, she wrote her number on the reverse, across the seal, and placed the envelope in a cardboard box. One by one, the other five girls followed suit, each placing her own number on the reverse of her envelope.

"Now that is settled." Paul announced. "The girls will retire to the utility room and wait for their number to be called to be introduced to their Master for the weekend and make their submission."

Yasmin ushered the girls from the lounge along a passage to the utility room at the rear of the house. As they proceeded, they passed the door that lead to the basement. It was here, in the 'Dungeon' that the girls would report when summoned, Yasmin explained to her. There was an air of nervous expectation in the room where the girls stood around, awaiting their number to be called. Melanie, being the only new one there for the first time, was even more nervous than the others. Yasmin informed her that the submission would be heard, both in this room and where the Masters waited, through loud speakers.

Her apprehension was not helped when Nicola sidled up to her and whispered. "I hope I don't get Hassan. He beats very hard and demands strange things at night. I don't know how Jenny puts up with him. She must love him very much."

"Oh!" Melanie whispered back. "I hope I don't get him either, then." She wondered what the 'strange things' could be that so clearly frightened the girl.

Further conversation was halted by a loud click from a loud speaker in the corner of the room, followed by a voice announcing, 'Slave number three'.

Jenny, giving the others a nervous smile, left the room. There was a pregnant silence as the remaining five girls looked at each other, apprehension clearly showing on their faces. Yasmin came close to Melanie and put a comforting arm round her shoulders. The silence was broken by another loud click from the loud speaker. Then they heard a swishing sound, which terminated in a sharp 'crack'.

"That was the cane," Yasmin whispered. Clearly, previous sessions had taught her to distinguish the sounds of each implement.

Twice more a report echoed in the room, each followed by a gasp. The next was followed by a cry of pain. Melanie counted silently to herself as another twelve reports sounded, followed by cries, which turned into screams, as Jenny was 'introduced' to her master for the weekend.

"Fifteen with the cane!" Yasmin said in her ear, rather unnecessarily Melanie thought.

Jenny was followed, at fifteen minute intervals, by Annette and Judy. According to Yasmin, they were dealt eighteen with the tawse and sixteen with the cane respectively. As each received their strokes, cries and screams rang round the room. Melanie sensed that Annette screamed sooner, and louder, than the others. Was she less experienced? Melanie was well used to a cane, tawse and switch being used on her, but had never been beaten with a birch. Had never actually seen one even! She prayed that she would not have to endure that, not for the first time that weekend.

"Number two," the voice from the loud speaker ordered. Nicola, who Melanie found out later was the youngest one present, being only just twenty-one years old, began to walk slowly to the door.

"Pray that I don't get the birch," she said over her shoulder as she left the room.

"That's the switch," Yasmin said, as a sharp report, followed by a loud gasp, echoed round the room a few minutes later.

Nicola only managed to take three more strokes before a shrill scream rang in the air. From then on she yelled and screamed as another fifteen strokes were laid on her buttocks. Now there were only Melanie and Yasmin remaining in the room.

The silence in the room was broken as the voice announced, 'Slave number four'.

Yasmin gave Melanie an extra tight hug and whispered. "Good luck. I know it's your first time but be brave and show them you can take it."

"Thank you," Melanie stuttered in reply as she disentangled herself and walked to the door. "I'll do my best."

With nervous steps, she descended to the basement and knocked on the Dungeon door. She heard a command to enter. She obeyed, closed the door behind her and sank to her knees. She shuddered as a sudden feeling of foreboding passed over her. Was she fated to be 'owned' by Hassan for the weekend?

"This is my lucky day," a voice said. A voice which Melanie now recognised as belonging to a man she had heard called James! She uttered an inward sigh of relief. She had been spared an encounter with Hassan on her first visit! She raised her eyes and looked at the bright blue eyes in the man's face. She shuddered as she saw the smile of pleasure on his mouth. He might not be Hassan but his expression warned her that he would make the best of being the first to have her.

"I prayed that you would be the one sent to me. It is always a pleasure to have a slave on her first attendance at our Meetings."

Melanie felt her legs trembling. She was unsure if she was expected to say anything. However, remembering what was in store for her, she determined to try and make her ordeal easier. "I hope Master will not be disappointed. I am only a novice, but I will do my best to please you," she said, as demurely as she could. She had decided that total submission was her best course.

"That remains to be seen," James said. "Stand and prepare yourself."

Slowly, as seductively as she could, Melanie rose and obeyed, putting the three items of her filmy costume in a bag with her number on it, one of several hanging from hooks on the wall. She stood, hands pressed to the outside of her thighs, trying to avoid his gaze as he looked her up and down. As she looked round the room, her eyes saw a wooden frame in the shape of two letter 'A's joined by cross pieces, the top one of which was heavily padded and covered with leather. This was still damp from the sweat of the girls who had preceded her to this room. It was over this, she knew, she would soon be ordered bend.

"Come," James ordered, pointing to a small table to one side, on which reposed the cardboard box.

Melanie approached the table and stood facing it. James,

at her side, put his arm round her, his hand cupping her breast while his fingers lightly fondled her nipple. To her horror, she felt her nipple harden under his touch.

"Take out the envelope with your number on it and remove the contents," he ordered, giving her nipple a slight pinch.

With trembling fingers Melanie obeyed, laying the three smaller envelopes on the table.

"Open the red one," He told her, moving now behind her and looking over her shoulder.

Melanie tore the envelope open and extracted the card from inside. Both of James's hands were now cupping her breasts and she felt her body begin to respond to his touch.

"The Queen of Diamonds," he read from the card as his fingers closed tight over her nipples. "That is twelve. Now open the green one."

Melanie, wishing that her body would not betray her so easily, opened the green envelope, hoping that fate would be kind to her and only reveal the lowest card, an eight.

"The ten of spades," James said as Melanie revealed the card. "That makes twenty-two!"

His hands slid down and round her until they now cupped her bottom cheeks. Melanie felt herself flinch at his touch. He began to stroke her bottom gently. Knowing that he would shortly be inflicting pain there, Melanie thought this a little sadistic.

"Now all we have to find out is which instrument you are to enjoy," he said, his mouth near her ear. "Which would you prefer, slave?"

"Whichever would please you most, Master," Melanie replied softly, nuzzling her neck against his cheek.

"There is one card for each of the cane, tawse and birch left," he said, pressing his hands harder against her bottom and sex lips. "The birch would decorate your behind nicely! Open the white envelope."

Melanie obeyed. The card fell on the table close to her and out of James's sight. The one word on it filled her with alarm as she remembered Nicola's words. She had drawn the birch, something that had never been used on her before, but it was Nicola's master, not her own, who would wield it. She silently prayed that he would find her performance satisfactory.

"Your wish has been granted, Master," Melanie whispered, trying to conceal the panic in her voice, as she held the card so that he could see it.

"This really is my lucky day!" James said, giving her buttocks a hard pat. "Go and bend over ready."

Thinking that it was far from her lucky day, Melanie turned and walked to the frame. Taking a deep breath, she bent over and gripped the legs of the frame tight. She wanted desperately to beg James not to beat her hard, but knew that she dared not.

She felt straps tightened round her wrists and ankles. She felt her legs tremble as she awaited her ordeal.

"You are forbidden to speak," James ordered.

Melanie heard him switch on the microphone that hung over the frame. Now it was her turn for her beating to be broadcast so that the others could hear. She raised her head and nearly disobeyed his order, as she saw him hold the birch in front of her face. The very sight sent waves of terror through her. A bundle of perhaps a dozen very thin, whippy, birch rods that were bound together at one end to form a handle! The vision disappeared. She heard a loud swish.

Thwack.

The birch rods lashed across the centre of her taut buttocks. She only just managed to hold back a yell of shock and pain as her head jerked up, her lips drawn back over her teeth. All the beatings she had so far endured had not prepared her for a first stroke that hurt so much. Neither had, it seemed to her, one been laid on with such terrible force. The rods had spread on impact, leaving a flaming band of pain in their wake.

Crack.

Another band of fire joined the first. Although she remained silent, except for a sharp hiss as her breath was drawn in between her teeth, she could not stop her buttocks clenching and unclenching frantically. She looked up, backwards over her shoulder, in time to see James raise the birch high over his shoulder and the smile on his lips. It was the last thing she was to see clearly.

Thwack.

The birch laced across her bottom, sending waves of searing pain through her cheeks. Her mouth fell open as a shrill cry of agony was wrenched from her. As her suffering body writhed on the leather bar, tears flooded her eyes.

Thwack.

The fourth stroke drew a deep groan of surrender from her throat as she felt her control slipping. She still had eighteen more strokes to come!

Crack.

Thwack.

The last of her control slipped away as these two strokes added their share of pain to her bottom. Her screams echoed round the room and from the loud speakers in other rooms in the house. Her young body writhed over the bar as the fire in her bottom turned into a furnace.

Thwack.

Crack.

Each stroke lifted her up on to her toes. Her screams echoed round the room. The birch hurt terribly, worse than a cane or switch.

Thwack.

Crack.

Thwack.

Three strokes, laid on in quick succession, wrung long shrill screams from the bent girl. Her body writhed on the bar as sweat streamed from her skin. She felt the arousal escalating in her belly as the furnace burning in her buttocks spread through her stomach to the whole of her body.

Melanie had tried to count the strokes as best she could and she realised with both relief, and dread, that she was now half way through her ordeal. The pain had passed any she had endured before, and this time she was not even being beaten as a punishment. Merely for the pleasure of the man wielding the birch.

James paused for a moment while he surveyed the girl's behind. His nature didn't allow him to feel pity, he was, after all a Master and she was merely a slave. Yet this girl, who was here for the first time and being thrashed by someone other than her own Master, was taking the thrashing quite well. He even thought of trying to buy her from Craig!

He returned to his position at her side. There was something else he had noticed. Her body was being sexually aroused by the birch! Instead of continuing with the beating, he held the birch against her throbbing cheeks and drew it slowly back and forth. He was rewarded as a groan of desire escaped her lips. He smiled and changed position until the birch was between her legs, sliding across her thighs and vulva. Immediately her body pressed back against the tormentor, and an even louder moan of desire came from her.

Thwack.

Crack.

Thwack.

As this latest stroke seared her cheeks, Melanie's body arched rigid, her head thrown back as she screamed both with pain and desire. Any hope of controlling her arousal flew through the window. The writhing of her sex over the bar, and the pain in her buttocks, had escalated her arousal to threatening heights. Only one thought now filled her pain racked mind. To hold back the orgasm at all costs!

Thwack.

Crack.

Even as she writhed and screamed, Melanie was fighting her hardest to contain the arousal that was on the verge of escalating into a shattering orgasm. Her first experience of the birch was playing havoc with her thoughts. Although it was in the hands of a stranger, it seemed to be teaching her the true meaning of slavery. She was being beaten by a stranger, solely for his pleasure. She knew she should revolt against this and the pain she was suffering, but the sheer dominance she was being subjected to was affecting her strongly. Was she, in fact, a real slave at heart?

The last six strokes of her ordeal lashed across her swollen and throbbing bottom. Sweat, mingled with the juices of her arousal seeped down her thighs, spread over her body and dropped from her pendant breasts to form pools on the floor.

At last, through the mist of pain, Melanie sensed James release her bonds and she sank, a quivering heap on the floor. James switched off the speaker.

"Your submission is completed," he said. "Get up and follow me."

"Thank you, Master, for my beating. I hope I was pleasing to Master," Melanie said through her sobs. She struggled to her feet stood facing him. Through her tear filled eyes, she saw him take a studded dog collar and fasten it round her neck. He attached a lead to it and led her from the room.

Waiting her turn upstairs, Yasmin had breathed a sigh of relief as Melanie's beating had progressed. She was sure that Hassan had been one of the earlier Masters to meet his slave and, if she was right, at least she was spared submitting to him. That the birch had now been put to use was another blessing. Used to corporal punishment as she was, the birch was the one implement above all that she feared, even more than the whip or cat o' nine tails, that Paul occasionally used on her.

Trying to ignore the waves of pain that flowed through her with every step, Melanie followed James up the stairs to another room. Here, the four men, with their beaten slaves kneeling at their side, were seated. Hassan was sitting with Annette kneeling at his side, her eyes red with weeping and her body still shuddering from her beating. Melanie sank to her knees in her place at the side of James who, also, was now seated. She glanced round at the other slaves. Each returned her gaze through pain filed eyes but with sympathy and compassion towards her. They had all seen as she crossed the room, that she had been badly thrashed with the birch, and were surprised to see a smile of happiness on her lips.

Melanie felt a twinge of jealousy however, as Craig rose and left the room. He had drawn the lovely Yasmin, and she knew that night he would enjoy the delights of her luscious body.

"Slave six," the words issued from the speaker.

All eyes were drawn to the speaker. There was a few minutes delay then a sharp report echoed, clearly defined as the sound of rattan striking taut bare flesh. Melanie listened as report after report echoed in the silence in the room. Yasmin cried out on the sixth and screamed on the tenth. Melanie counted and, as the tally passed the twenty mark, she began to wonder what was going on down there. What she did not know was that Yasmin had drawn two kings, twenty-six for their face value plus four extra for a pair. The reports only stopped when Melanie's count reached thirty. Some minutes later, Craig returned to the room, followed by a still sobbing Yasmin.

The submissions having been completed the slaves were ordered to go and clean themselves and then to prepare and serve lunch. The afternoon passed pleasantly. The naked slaves serving the men as required. They joined in the various games that were played to pass the time, nothing strenuous or likely to aggravate the pain in their behinds. At eight o'clock, when the supper things had been cleared away, Hassan ordered Annette to him. He attached the lead to the collar round her neck ordered her to go down on her hands and knees. Thus, to her shame, he led her like a dog to her room.

Although Melanie felt reluctance at having to submit sexually to anyone other than Craig, she followed James, also on a lead attached to the collar round her neck, apparently willingly from the room up the stairs, and into the bedroom allocated to her. To her surprise and pleasure, James, whilst still being masterful with her, treated her body with respect. As the evening passed into night, he used her body for his pleasure. To her relief, he demanded nothing other than the conventional sex that she was used to and, as their stamina flagged, even allowed her to enjoy several orgasms before finally settling down to sleep.

When she awoke in the morning, she opened her eyes to find that the bedclothes had been pulled off her naked body and James leaning on his elbow regarding her with a smile on his face.

You really are something," he said softly. "Craig is a very lucky man to own you. I wonder if he would agree to sell you to me."

Melanie could hardly believe what she had heard. It had never crossed her mind that she could be bought and sold like a commodity.

"He wouldn't sell me," she said. "For one thing, I wouldn't agree to it. I'm not a piece of furniture that can be bought and sold."

"A slave has no say in it if her Master wishes to dispose of her in that way," James replied, his voice sounding angry. "You are a slave and must obey his wishes."

"That is one wish I would never, under any circumstances obey!" Melanie shouted back at him.

"So there is rebellion in the slave is there?" James answered. "Perhaps I should inform your Master of what you have said and see what he would do about it." Melanie shuddered at the venom he put into the words. "Now, run my bath and go and help in the kitchen."

She quickly obeyed and was soon dressed in her costume, having also washed herself and applied her make up. She hurried down the stairs, grateful to escape from the bedroom. The conversation had taken a turn she did not want to think any more about.

She helped the other girls prepare breakfast and, while they waited for the Masters to descend to the dining room, sat around the kitchen table and took their own meal. Melanie sat next to Annette and was disturbed to see that the girl was shuddering and close to tears.

"Whatever is the matter, Annette?" she asked concernedly.

"I hate Hassan, he's a perverted ogre," the girl stammered her reply. "Even if I am whipped until I have no skin on my back, I will never submit to him again."

After being begged to explain Annette told her about the previous evening. Apparently Hassan had made her behave like a dog, a 'bitch' as she said he called her. He made her crawl round the bedroom on her hands and knees, bark like a dog, eat dog food and lap up water from a bowl. When he tired of this, he made her kneel on the end of the bed, her bottom raised in the air, and rammed his cock into her anus, something that had never been done before. She said she felt humiliated and defiled. When asked why she didn't refuse, there and then, Annette said that Hassan had

115

threatened to have her whipped in front of everyone that morning and that he would demand the right to apply the whip. She was terrified that if he did he would beat her so hard that her back would be scarred for life.

It was after breakfast that, crossing the hall, Melanie encountered Hassan. He and Jenny were dressed in outdoor clothes and appeared to be on the point of leaving. Melanie hurried across the hall but, just as she thought she had made it to the kitchen door, she heard her name called. It was Hassan. Scared to do otherwise, she halted, turned and approached him.

"I am disappointed that I did not draw you to serve me this visit. Maybe I will be luckier next time," he said.

"There will be no next time, as far as you're concerned," Melanie replied, still incensed by what she had been told about him. Her disgust with him was so great that she completely ignored the instructions that a slave should kneel when addressed by a Master.

"What do you mean by that, slut?" Hassan's face had changed to a deep red in anger.

"I mean that you will never have me as your slave or anything else!" she yelled at him. "I know what you did to Annette. You're a pervert and a sadist with a twisted mind. I hope you rot in hell! I will never submit to a disgusting beast like you!"

Hassan's face turned even redder at her words. "One day, you slut, you will pay for those insults. Unfortunately I have to leave right away but, be warned, at the next Meeting I shall demand not only that you be thoroughly whipped for your insolence but I shall also demand the right to apply the whip. Come slave!" Addressing this last order to Jenny, he marched through the front door leaving Jenny, who clearly looked terrified at Hassan's outburst, to pick up his bags and follow him.

Melanie watched him go. She had lost control of her

temper and was thankful that he had to leave then, or he would, she was sure, have demanded that she suffer for her crime there and then. She shuddered as she thought of having to strip naked in front of everyone and have Hassan lash her back with a whip. Apart from the fact that she wanted her own Master to be the first to take a whip to her, the ferocity with which Hassan would have lashed her made her legs shake with terror. Somehow, she must persuade Craig never to attend a Meeting when Hassan would be present.

The morning passed slowly. Fearing that in her behaviour with James the previous evening might have been reported to the Masters, she went about her duties with the constant threat that she might be brought to account for her actions and any minute she expected to be summoned to atone for her behaviour. She tried to console herself that, although they would all watch, it would be her Craig that would apply the whip to her back. To her surprise, and relief, nothing happened.

On the way home, Melanie sat beside Craig, her bottom, which was still very sore from the birching, hurt with every bump in the road. But Craig had heard about the ruckus in the hall and demanded that she explained herself, which she did, although she was unable to control her voice and hide the terrible dread of the threat Hassan had made.

"You little fool!" Craig exploded. "If he attends the next Meeting, you will be put on trial for your conduct. If he demands that he whips you, I will not be able to persuade the others to refuse him. I did not know details of who was to be there this time and, if I had, I would have warned you to keep a civil tongue in your head. But you know how a slave should behave, even under provocation. The matter is out of my hands."

"Can't you refuse to go next time, if he is going to be there?" she asked.

117

"No. To do so would bar us from attending any more of their Meetings ever again, or those of any other group. Word gets around quickly. Anyway, I enjoyed myself immensely and the other girls looked equally appealing."

Melanie was stunned at his words. He seemed quite prepared to let Hassan loose with a whip on her body just so that he could take his pleasure with the bodies of the other slaves present. A dreadful silence prevailed during the remainder of the journey home and the subject was not mentioned again by either of them. Remembering what he had said, however, spurred Melanie to exercising all her charms to ensure she kept his interest focused on her.

CHAPTER 6.

After that weekend party, Craig made no mention of the events in which they had both been involved. Melanie couldn't help feeling jealous thinking how her Master had enjoyed beating Yasmin and sampling delights of her voluptuous body. All that she was sure of was that he had thrashed her well and truly with the cane. She had seen the evidence on the girl's buttocks! Melanie dreaded that he would make her attend another such Meeting. It would be just her luck for Hassan to be there and she knew she could not face having him whip her. It would be the one and only time that she would revoke the willingness of her submission.

Her fears were allayed, however, when Craig ascertained some weeks later, from one of his contacts that Hassan had been recalled to his own country and would not be returning. Melanie felt a great relief when Craig imparted this news to her. She had escaped the whipping she knew he would have made her take. However, her elation was short lived. It appeared that Hassan had not taken Jenny with him and, since she was without a master, Paul had asked Craig to take charge of her until a suitable Master could be found or keep her for himself. It seemed that Jenny was distraught at having been left behind. It seemed that she had really loved Hassan, whether this was in spite of, or because of, the way he had treated her Melanie never could decide.

Jenny soon fitted in with her new position, both in the house and office. She was subject to the same rules, and punishments, as Melanie and Craig had ordered that when one was punished the other must watch. The one thing that she found hard to accept was Craig's insistence that he used Jenny in his bed whenever he felt the desire for her body. For some time, Melanie was to suffer torments those nights she lay on her own bed, knowing that Craig was enjoying Jenny's lovely body. But strangely, she felt no antagonism towards either Craig or Jenny. She just had to hope that what had started out as a temporary arrangement did not become a permanent one.

In the meantime, Melanie fretted that she might end up losing Craig and racked her mind to think of some way to bind herself to him even more tightly. Suddenly she remembered something she had read or heard somewhere. What was it? She thought and thought and eventually she remembered. 'A woman does not know herself to be a true slave until she has felt the whip across her back'. That was it! But would it work in reverse? Would Craig keep her with him permanently once he had used a whip on her? She had to contrive that Craig did just that. Whip her across her back and make her his true slave! But he had not yet used a whip and did not seem to be inclined to do so.

A week passed during which Melanie made sure she was on her best behaviour. She was determined at all costs, not to deserve a beating since she knew Jenny would be ordered to watch. It had been bad enough being beaten by Alex with Jenny watching, but she had managed to keep her sexual arousal under covers so that they did not see. When James beat her at the Meeting, there was no one watching and, anyway, it had been a stranger. She was only too well aware that she would be unable to control, or hide, her body's reaction when it was Craig, her own Master, laying on the strokes.

In the event, her fears were groundless. At the end of Jenny's first week in the house, Melanie was crossing the hall when Craig emerged from his study. Jenny was nowhere in sight.

"Follow me," Craig ordered, and led her down to the Correction Room.

Melanie was concerned. If she was to be beaten, why had he not ordered her to prepare herself and report to him there? They entered the Correction Room and Craig ordered her to stand behind the judgement seat, which she did. She watched as he switched on all the lights and the video recorders, just as if she was to be flogged. He sat in the chair with a red book - her punishment record book? – face down, on the small table at his side. She heard the hall clock strike the hour. Immediately, there was a knock on the door and, in response to his command, Jenny entered.

She closed the door behind her, approached the Judgement Seat keeping her eyes demurely lowered and knelt. Melanie silently caught her breath. Jenny was following the same procedure that she did when summoned there for a beating. Craig must have taught her the routine unbeknown to her. He picked up the red book, opened it, and looked down at the girl kneeling before him.

"Slave." His stern voice broke the silence. "You are guilty of disobedience and have been summoned here for punishment. Prepare."

Slowly and seductively, Jenny rose, discarded her costume and knelt, this time opening her knees wide.

"You are to be beaten with the switch across your buttocks," Craig, his voice still stern, pronounced. "Proceed."

Jenny gracefully rose, turned, and walked to the wall where the implements hung. She took down the switch and returned again kneeling with her knees spread and the switch lying across her upraised hands.

"Disobedience is a serious matter and will be dealt with accordingly. You are sentenced to twenty strokes. Since this is your first punishment, a further ten strokes will be added for my pleasure. Position."

Jenny thanked the switch for the punishment it was about to mete out to her, kissed it lovingly and raised her hands towards Craig. When he had taken it from her hands, she rose and walked to the narrow bar and bent over. Craig secured her in position by her wrists and ankles, retrieved the switch and took up his position to her left, holding the switch lightly against her trembling buttocks.

"To what punishment are you sentenced slave?" Craig's stern voice broke the silence that had descended in the room.

"Twenty hard strokes of the switch across my bare bottom, Master, followed by a further ten strokes for your pleasure," Jenny replied, her voice betrayed the nervousness that was causing her legs to tremble.

Melanie watched the proceedings with a strong feeling of jealousy. She was watching her Master with another girl, and following the same procedure as she did. It was almost like watching one of the films of one of her own punishments! She suddenly let out a stifled gasp. To her amazement, and concern, she had suddenly realised that the spectacle before her was causing her own body to become aroused.

"For what offence are you to be punished slave?" Craig demanded.

"For disobedience, Master," Jenny replied.

As she uttered the last word, Craig's arm rose high in the air then swiftly descended, lacing the switch across Jenny taut buttocks with a resounding report. A suppressed gasp escaped the girl's clenched teeth. Melanie remembered that, at the weekend Meeting, Jenny had only taken three stokes of the cane before crying out. She had heard later in the day, that Hassan liked his slave to scream early on and Jenny had not had to learn otherwise. Melanie saw that Jenny's hands were gripping the end of the bar so tight her knuckles shone white, and that the girl's buttocks were clenching and unclenching as she absorbed the pain.

Three more stokes rained down on the white canvas of

Jenny's behind, each leaving a livid red line in its wake. Still Jenny remained silent except for a loud gasp each time the switch cut into her cheeks. The fifth stroke wrung a cry of agony and distress from the bent slave. From then on, her cries became louder with each stroke until, as the ninth cut into her sore bottom, an agonised scream echoed round the room.

Melanie watched transfixed as the full thirty strokes were applied. Jenny's screams grew louder and more prolonged as the pain of the beating escalated and spread from her buttocks to the remainder of her body. Melanie was also conscious that, watching the flogging was escalating the arousal in her own body and it was only by exerting strict control that she prevented her fingers from delving into her own sex. Surely this was not right? Although she had seen the marks on Julia's bottom where Alex had beaten her and the other girls' behinds after the submission session at the weekend Meeting, it was the first time she had seen another girl actually being beaten. How could watching another girl thrashed cause her own sex to respond as if it were she bent over the bar and being flogged?

As Craig replaced the switch and resumed his seat, Melanie looked hard at the thrashed behind. The once pale surface of Jenny's skin was covered by a mass of livid raised weals. Her eyes were drawn to the girls sex pouch, nestling between her spread legs and saw that the lips were wide open and juices were seeping down the inside of the thighs. Jenny's body had also become aroused by the thrashing! And Melanie had always been embarrassed in thinking she was the only one to respond in that fashion.

"You may release the slave," Craig said, turning towards her.

Melanie obeyed, releasing Jenny's ankles then her wrists. Jenny let out a low moan as she straightened up. She walked gingerly to where Craig sat and sank to her knees. In a voice still shaking from her beating, she thanked her Master for her punishment. As Melanie had been taught to do, Jenny kept her hands away from her buttocks until she had closed the door behind her.

Fifteen minutes later, Jenny appeared in the lounge to where Craig and Melanie had retired after the punishment. She had stopped sobbing, had cleaned herself and repaired her make up, and the only visible evidence that she had been thrashed were the redness around her eyes where she had cried and the marks on her backside. The two girls continued with their duties.

That night, neither of them was summoned to Craig's bed. Melanie lay in her own bed and, before she fell asleep, thought over what had occurred that afternoon. It was a relief to discover that Jenny, like herself, became sexually aroused when under punishment. It would not now be necessary for Melanie to hide her reaction when her turn came. Craig had made no comment about Jenny yelling so soon during the thrashing but, she was sure, he would not delay in telling her that she must do better in the future.

The one thought that did give Melanie concern was that Jenny had already told her that Hassan had taken a proper whip to her, not only across her back and buttocks, but across the front of her body as well. A fact of which Craig would already be aware! How long, Melanie wondered would it be before he took a whip to Jenny? One thing Melanie was sure of was that she did not want it to be Jenny that he first took a whip to. That was her prerogative, being his first slave! The phrase she had recalled about a girl not knowing true slavery until she felt the lash kept going through her mind. She had been Craig's slave now for eighteen months and he had still not whipped her, and she wanted to be a true slave for her Master. Then, thinking of a whip, she remembered that, if she was found to be displeasing at any future Meeting, she would be whipped for it. But she did not want her first encounter with a whip to occur in front of a crowd of virtual strangers. With this thought in her mind she fell asleep.

In the days that followed, Melanie mulled over these thoughts, wondering what she could do about it. She must, somehow, make sure that Craig whipped her before he did Jenny and also before she earned a whipping at a Meeting. An idea began to form in her mind. A daring idea that frightened her terribly! She let the idea germinate in her mind and in the end decided that she would act on it. A month before Craig's birthday, he had to go away for a few days on business. It gave Melanie a chance to put into action the plan that had twirled round in her mind for days. Throwing caution to the winds and risking a terrible punishment, she took a day off work and journeyed to London.

She had seen the whips hanging in the Punishment Room but was aware that he had used them on his previous slaves. She wanted a new one, that had not been used on those others, to be used for her first whipping.

Arriving in London, she set out for a certain area where, as she had gleaned from a magazine she had seen at Paul's house, one could buy instruments and garments of a S & M nature. She had secretly saved some money and determined to buy Craig a whip to add to his collection. He would regard her unauthorised absence from the office with extreme anger. Perhaps that, and being presented with yet another whip, might induce him to use it on her. The flogging she would receive would be terribly severe, she knew, but she just had to precipitate the event somehow.

She visited several shops, suffering terrible embarrassment as the male assistants smirked as she explained what she required, before she found one that sold exactly what she wanted. It was easier there, for the only assistant in the shop at the time was a young woman.

Melanie knew she wanted a whip but, on looking round the shop, she saw many items that she thought Craig would like but she couldn't afford them all. Once she had confided that it was she that the various things would be used on, the young woman was very helpful. Eventually she chose a long lashed whip with a beautifully engraved handle depicting a naked woman, tied to a post, being flogged with a whip. The very sight of this sent pangs of fear through her but it was a lovely whip and her body began to juice just at the thought of the lash biting into her soft body. To this, she added a blindfold, and a leather ball gag, things that she was sure, Craig did not already possess.

She was about to pay for these when she caught sight of a cat-o-nine tails hanging in a corner. She took it down and looked at it closely. This was one type of whip, she knew, that did not hang on the wall in the Correction Room. She was tempted, especially as she had never heard Jenny say that one had been used on her although Hassan had frequently used a single lash whip. But she was a bit apprehensive about it. She was sure that, once in Craig's hands he would not be able to resist the temptation to use it hard on her soft body. What if it left scars on her? She would not be so attractive to him then!

Her fears were soon allayed. The assistant, guessing the doubt in her mind, took her into a back room. She explained that the whip was especially designed for use on a female body, and that the individual thongs were suppler than the heavier whips that were for use on a male slave. It would generate extreme pain but, even if blood was drawn, it would not leave permanent scars. When Melanie still seemed doubtful, the girl told her that her boy friend had caught her with another man two days previously and had punished her with a similar whip, twenty-five very hard lashes that had made her scream terribly. She turned away from Melanie and removed her blouse. Her back was a mass of hard raised ridges over heavy bruising, but nowhere had the skin been broken. This decided Melanie and she added it to the implements on the counter.

Clutching the large parcel of her purchases, she left the shop and made her way back to the station. On arriving home, she hid her purchases away until she could present them to Craig on his birthday. All that remained now was to ensure that she was not beaten in the meantime. Once he found out that she had taken a day out of the office without permission, she was sure that her desire to stand at the post for a whipping would be fulfilled.

Craig's flight back landed at four in the afternoon and, an hour later, the slaves heard his car pull up outside the front door. Jenny and Melanie, both dressed in their costumes and carefully made up stood waiting in the hall as he opened the door and entered. To their utter astonishment, he was not alone. A woman, who Melanie estimated at somewhere in her early forties, accompanied him. He closed the door and stood looking at the sight that awaited his return, his two slaves, dressed in their costumes, kneeling submissively in the hall.

He introduced the woman as Ayesha and ordered the slaves to prepare coffee and bring it to the lounge. The girls departed to the kitchen to carry out his order. As they worked they wondered who the woman was and why she was there. They entered the lounge, served the two their coffees and knelt at the side of the room awaiting further orders. Craig and Ayesha talked together for a few minutes, then Craig ordered the slaves to come and kneel in front of him. As they obeyed, the woman rose and stood behind his chair.

"As from the end of next week," Craig began. "Certain changes will take place. The business has expanded considerably of late and I am promoting Colin as the Office Manager. I will be spending more time at home here, concentrating on the more important accounts. Margaret and Sylvia will take over your duties in the office and you will spend the week teaching them the ropes. From them on, you will both be here with me in the house where you will be my personal secretaries."

He paused to let this sink in then continued. "Ayesha is to be my housekeeper. She will occupy the Granny Flat attached to the east side of the house. You will, under no circumstances, enter that area. There is a bell on the connecting door and, if you need to see her when she is off duty, you will ring the bell. You two will assist Ayesha in the housework. I have told her that she is to be obeyed in the same way as you obey me and you will treat her with respect and call her 'Madam'. She will be strict with you and has my authority to administer up to six strokes of the strap across your behinds for any small infringement. You will submit without question. Part of her duties will be to teach you to dance for me and my guests' entertainment. You will also report to her immediately after a beating. She has a special lotion which, although it does not reduce the pain, will make the marks disappear more quickly." Again Craig paused. Melanie and Jenny glanced sideways at each other. Both had a wondering look on their faces as they digested the new order of things.

The following two weeks were frantic for all of them. During the day, Melanie and Jenny passed on their work to the other girls. The evenings were taken up with getting to know the duties Ayesha would require them to do. She also had them each make a couple of working shifts. These consisted solely of a piece of gingham material that fitted like a loose tube from the top of their breasts, where it was held in place by a draw ribbon at the top, to just below their buttocks. These they would wear when working about the house to save their costumes from getting dirty or damaged.

The two girls soon came to accept Ayesha's presence and, in return, found the woman easy to get along with. She was not too critical and allowed for a few mistakes in that first week. Consequently, neither girl had to bend for the strap. They had seen this hanging on one of the kitchen walls. Whilst they had no fear of the strap, believing that Ayesha would not be able to muster anywhere near the force that Craig could, neither wanted to bend for it. To be beaten, even a few strokes with the strap, by a woman would be too humiliating to contemplate.

One evening, Craig was working in his study and Ayesha summoned the slaves to the lounge. Here she ordered them to strip. She carefully examined their bodies, testing for muscle development, suppleness and flexibility. Then she made them stand and then walk in a circle round the room while she stood in the centre and watched them. After a few minutes, she began to instruct them how to improve their posture, to walk more seductively and submissively.

"That is how you will stand and walk in future," she told them. "I will be watching you and any slipping back into your old ways and I will use the strap on you." She smiled to herself at the concerned looks that passed between her pupils. "Your bodies are not yet quite supple enough to dance properly, so we will start exercising as of now. Once you can move in a flowing, seductive manner befitting a dancing girl then, and only then, will I begin the dancing lessons. But, be warned, any slow progress will be rewarded with the strap."

The exercises began immediately. Each day for the next two weeks, they went through one exercise after another until their bodies ached and muscles that they had not known they possessed hurt painfully. Each evening, they spent an hour at this and, gradually the stiffness wore off and the routines became easier.

Friday of the second week, their final day in the office,

came to an end and the two girls bade farewell to the rest of the staff. Although they knew that, from then on, they would be total slaves, there was a sense of relief at the departure. Both of them had been in constant fear that, by bending over too far, or some other mischance, they would expose their bottoms to the others in the office. Not only would it be seen that they wore no undergarments, but, if they had recently been beaten, the marks would also be on view.

On arriving home, Melanie had one task to perform. The next day was Craig's birthday and she had to wrap the presents she had bought. This had to be done without Craig, Ayesha or Jenny seeing. It was with great difficulty, and careful scheming, that this was eventually accomplished and the parcel hidden behind the furniture in the dining room. She intended to present this to her Master after breakfast in the morning. It had been an exhausting week for Craig and he retired to bed without summoning either girl to attend him.

Melanie lay on her bed and, in the moments before sleep overcame her, she thought of the morrow and the terrible retribution she would pay for her absence from the office that day. She only hoped that her dream would come true and that her Master would use one of the whips for her punishment. A whipping that would not only punish her but would also, if what she had come to believe was true, teach her the real meaning of her slavery! She also hoped that once Crag had taken a whip to her body it would strengthen her position and drive away the ever present fear that Craig might tire of her one day and dispose of her.

Morning came, bringing with it a warm sunny day. Melanie took extra care with her toilet that morning and descended the stairs. Ayesha dispatched Jenny with the Master's morning tea and then the three of them quickly ate their breakfast. Melanie, her stomach fluttering with excitement and trepidation, ate very little.

Craig descended the stairs and went into the dining room, where the two slaves, dressed in their costumes awaited him. He sat down and opened the morning post that lay at the side of his place. He read this as he ate his breakfast. There were several private letters and some birthday cards which he put to one side. As he at last turned to his final cup of coffee, Melanie realised her time had come. She retrieved the parcel from where she had hidden it, approached the table and knelt at his side, the parcel laying across her upraised hands.

"Happy Birthday, Master," she said demurely, silently praying that her gift would achieve her designs.

A mixed look of surprise and anger crossed his face as he looked at the parcel – surprise at the unexpected present and anger that his slave had spoken before asking permission. But he was in a cheerful mood and let the latter pass. He took the parcel from her hands and began to unwrap it. The expression on his face turned to astonishment as he, one by one, unwrapped the manacles, ball gag, blindfold and, finally the two whips. Carefully, he placed them to one side and turned to Melanie.

"What do you intend the whips for?" he asked. The question seemed stupid, their purpose was obvious, but he was taken by surprise.

"For my Master to use on me!" Melanie answered softly, a slight quiver of nervousness in her voice. "I read or heard somewhere that a girl does not know the true meaning of her slavery until her back has felt the kiss of a whip. I hoped my Master would teach me to be a true slave."

"Very thoughtful of you!" Craig replied. "But where on earth did you get them?"

The question Melanie knew was sure to be asked! Would her answer produce the result for which she wished?

Slowly, hesitantly, she told him of her trip to London and of the shop where she had bought the items.

A stunned silence filled the room as the smile on Craig's face vanished as it turned red with anger. "Do you mean to tell me that you took a day out of the office without permission?" he shouted at her. "If I remember correctly, your very first thrashing was for leaving the office without permission." He stared hard at his trembling slave. "And I suppose you involved Jenny to cover up for you?"

"No, Master. I told her I had your permission to leave the office on your business," Melanie answered. She knew she was making her position worse by the minute, but she was not going to let Jenny take any of the blame.

"So!" Craig's voice sounded even angrier. "You added lying to your offence. Birthday or no Birthday, you will suffer for that. You will report to the Correction Room at eleven o'clock." He turned to Jenny. "You and Ayesha will report there at five minutes to the hour." With that, picking up his presents, he marched from the room.

Jenny and Ayesha both looked at Melanie in horror. Jenny had never seen Craig so angry before. Shaking her head in disbelief, she followed the older woman from the room. Melanie stood for a moment. She wondered if she had gone too far this time. That she was in for a terrible punishment there was no doubt. But had her scheme worked? Would her Master do as she had intended and use one of the whips on her and teach her the meaning of true slavery? Or would he, knowing her desire, deliberately beat her unmercifully with one of the other implements at his command? She prayed not! In about an hour and a half, she would find out. She shook these thoughts from her head and carried on with her duties.

The other two did not mention her offence or her ordeal to come until a quarter to eleven. She was in the kitchen helping Ayesha when the woman turned to her.

"You had better go and get ready, Melanie. Come and see me afterwards."

Melanie made her way to her room, where she ensured that her appearance was perfect. She visited the toilet and emptied her bladder and walked from her room. She nearly stumbled as she made her way down the stairs and stood, outside the Correction Room. She felt terrified yet there was an element of excitement as she wondered which whip, if any, her Master would use. As the hall clock struck the hour, she knocked on the door and, on Craig's summons entered, closing the door behind her. She walked as seductively as her screaming nerves would allow and stopped in front of the Judgement seat. As she gracefully dropped to her knees, she saw Jenny and Ayesha standing behind her Master, with very concerned looks on their faces.

"You are guilty of extreme disobedience, slave," Craig told her. "To which offence is added lying and usurping my authority to cover up your crime. You have expressed a wish to be taught the true meaning of slavery and this will now be done. You are to be whipped. With both of the whips you presented to me for that purpose. Prepare."

Melanie had felt the blood drain from her face at his pronouncement. She hadn't bargained for both whips to be used at the same session. She slowly rose to her feet and reached up to remove the veil. She was so frightened and nervous that her fingers would not release the clips from her ears.

"Jenny," Craig said, angry at her fumbling. "Strip the slave, or we will be here all day."

Jenny gently removed the items of the costume and hung them over her arm. Melanie turned, walked to the wall and took down both whips from where they had been hung on two new hooks. She returned and knelt before her Master, spreading her knees wide and holding the whips up on the palms of her hands.

"In view of the seriousness of your offence, you are to be punished with ten lashes of the single thong whip across your back and ten across your buttocks, followed by six lashes across your back and six across your buttocks with the cat o' nine tails. Proceed."

A gasp of horror came from behind her Master as Jenny heard the sentence. She knew Melanie had never been whipped before and her first experience of one was to be a terrible ordeal.

Melanie felt her hands shaking as the enormity of her punishment sank in. She was to take thirty two lashes, and twelve of those were to be with the 'cat'. She swallowed hard to steady her nerves.

"Master," she said, her voice trembling. "Your slave thanks the whips for the lesson in obedience they are about to teach her and also for making me into a true slave."

She kissed the whips lovingly and raised her arms towards her Master. She felt

the whips taken from her and rose to her feet. She turned and began walking towards the whipping post.

"No!" she heard her Master call out. "Go to the frame. Since you are so eager for the lash, you may see yourself whipped."

Melanie changed direction and walked towards the uprights. As she approached them she saw that an added refinement had been added. In the centre of them, a thin metal post stood upright and as she got near she realised this reached up to the middle of her thighs. She wondered why that had been fixed there. She halted in front of this and looked at the mirrors on the wall in front of her. She saw herself, a naked slave with fear in her eyes, reflected in the mirrors. As Craig approached, she raised her arms towards the corners of the frame. Craig halted behind her, crouched and attached her ankle cuffs to a ring set in the floor. Then he took her wrists and attached their cuffs to short chains hanging from the corners of the frame. Then she found out the purpose if the post. What she had not noticed were two leather straps fixed to the sides of the post. Craig pulled these round her thighs and buckled them together. She shuddered as she tried to wriggle but found she was firmly held against the post. He moved to her front and, parting it behind her, pulled her hair forward to drape down her chest.

Melanie could see her stretched body in the mirror, her breasts pulled upwards by the tension in her arms. She began to tremble with terror as she saw his reflection as he moved behind her and shook the lash loose. As his arm rose her small hands gripped the rings on the ends of the chains to which her wrist cuffs were attached tightly. In dreadful slow motion, she saw the lash approach then lost sight of it. Immediately there was a heavy impact across her back that drove the air from her lungs in a loud 'Woosh', stifling the scream that rose in her throat. Her body was thrust forward, thrusting her buttocks out backwards and it was across these that the next stroke curled. This time a piercing scream echoed round the room. Two lines of intense agony burned in her body. She had never hurt so much so early on in a punishment and her ordeal had only just started.

Crack.

Crack.

Her back and bottom each received another stroke, each one followed by a shrill scream as she tried to writhe under the impact. Melanie felt sweat break out all over her body and being strung up in the frame with a whip cutting into her had already aroused her body. The next stroke, across her back, curled round her side and the end of the lash cut into her stretched breast, right across the nipple and was quickly followed by one across her buttocks which, in turn, curled round her hip and the end of the thong sank into her already swollen sex lips. The next two strokes mirrored the previous ones, but Craig had changed to a back handed stroke and the thong curled round her from the other side.

Despite the terrible pain that seared through her, she was still silently counting the strokes. A groan escaped her as she realised she had, so far, only had half her sentence with the single lash and there was still the 'cat' to come. The two things she had decided she must avoid were to lose consciousness or orgasm before the full whipping had been completed. Through her tears she could see her reflection in the mirror and the angry red weals where the lash had curled round and bit into her breasts and belly.

As her Master continued to flog her writhing body, the agony that seared through her escalated. She screamed each time the lash struck, sometimes across her back, at others into her buttocks, sinking into a loud moaning and mewing in the intervals between each. Whilst she was aware of the arousal she was trying hard to contain, her mind filled with visions of a helpless slave girl of olden times being flogged with a cruel whip by her Master or one of his minions. In each, the slave girl was herself.

Having lost count, she was unaware of the twentieth stroke cutting into her pain racked bottom until no more blows fell. Jenny, already prepared on her Master's orders, hurried to stand in front of the sobbing slave and began to bathe her face with a cold wet cloth. Gradually, Melanie brought herself under some control.

"Is it over?" she asked feebly.

"You still have twelve with the 'cat' to come," Jenny whispered. "You're doing very well, be brave for a little longer. It'll soon be all over."

"Enough, Jenny!" Craig called out. "Return to your position."

Reluctantly, Jenny obeyed.

Melanie, whose eyes were now clear of tears, saw,

reflected in the mirror, her Master standing behind her, the 'cat' in his hand with its lashes hanging loose. She could not suppress a groan of despair at the vision. How could her young body endure a further whipping with that dreadful implement. For a fleeting moment, she regretted having been stupid, not only to buy the things but to have committed three unforgivable offences in the process. These thoughts were driven from her mind as she saw him raise his arm, she screwed her eyes shut and gripped the rings even tighter. This was what she had desired for so long. In her mind, the single lash had already banished any residual thoughts of being a free woman from her mind and ensured that, from then on, she would only ever think of herself as nothing but a slave. Now the 'cat' would ensure the permanence of her transformation.

Thwack.

The force of the impact drove her body hard against the post which separated her thighs cruelly. Her mouth opened wide in a soundless scream and her lips drew back over her teeth in a spasm of agony. She was unable to scream as the air in her lungs was forced through her open mouth. The thongs had spread on impact, cutting into the weals left by the single lash, causing a wide sheet of fire to explode in her back. She lost the strength in her legs which, had she not been stretched to the limit of her body, would have collapsed under her. The next stroke curled round her tortured buttocks, flinging her body forwards as far as it could go. This time it was her sex mound that caught the ends of the thongs making the arousal in her belly soar.

Thwack.

Thwack.

Two more strokes added to the agony in her back and buttocks. Her legs were no longer supporting her and her body had sunk down until the top of the metal post pressed up onto her sex. On the second, her pubes had hit the post with force and she kept her body pressed hard against the metal, grinding her sex, as two more lashes added their share to her suffering. She had gone beyond screaming. Now the only sounds she made were gasps as the leathers struck and moans and grunts of desire as her writhing against the post added fuel to her arousal.

Four more lashes rained down across her back and bottom to complete her punishment. As the thongs on the final stroke cut into the fire raging in her bottom, she let out a loud scream. Not a scream of pain but one of ecstasy as her arousal soared into the most blinding series of orgasms she had ever experienced and she sank into oblivion.

Ayesha and Jenny had watched the flogging in silence. They both knew Melanie had never been whipped before and had been appalled at the severity of the punishment when Craig had pronounced it. Jenny recalled that not even Hassan had been that harsh on her the first time he had taken a whip to her. That Melanie had remained conscious throughout the beating astounded them. Jenny, watching as Melanie ground her sex against the post as she took the 'cat' wished there had been such a post for her to relieve her agony on when she had been whipped.

Craig waited until Melanie recovered consciousness before ordering her release. Jenny unshackled Melanie's ankles then her waist. As she did so, she had a close look at her back and buttocks. Only in a few places had the skin been broken and thin trickles of red seeped out to mingle with the sweat that covered her skin. Jenny tried to support her as she unclasped her wrists but Melanie sank down to her knees. Ever so slowly she turned and began to crawl towards the Judgement Seat where Craig had resumed his place. Melanie's eyes were clouded in pain and she whimpered with each movement, but the others clearly saw the contented expression on her face and the quivering smile on her lips. She halted in front of her Master.

In a trembling voice, she began to speak. "I thank the whips for my punishment," she said. "And I thank my Master for teaching me my true slavery. I am yours to do with as you wish."

"I trust the whipping has taught you obedience, " Craig answered, then turned his head to look at Ayesha and Jenny standing behind him. "You may take the slave away and see to her. She is to report to the lounge in half an hour."

Melanie was helped to her feet by the two women and, stumbling with the pain, walked slowly from the room. They took her upstairs to her room where they made her lie, face down, on her bed. While Ayesha went to get the cream, Jenny gently bathed Melanie's back and bottom with a cold cloth. Gradually the whipped girl's sobbing and moaning quietened down. She raised her eyes to her sister slave.

"Am I badly marked?" she asked hesitantly. Her one fear was that the whip would scar her soft body and make her less desirable to her Master.

"Your body is well marked," Jenny replied gently. "But, although you're bleeding a bit, none of the lashes have cut you deep enough to leave permanent marks."

Melanie breathed a sigh of relief. Now that her worst fears were unfounded, she felt ready to talk.

"Did I take it well enough to please my Master, do you think?"

"You were very brave," Jenny replied. "I am sure the Master was pleased with your performance. How do you feel, apart from very painful, now that you've been taught to be a real slave?"

"Wonderful," Melanie replied. "At the beginning, I just cursed myself for buying those whips and wanted to beg him to stop. Then, as the pain built up, in my mind I saw myself like a slave of olden times being beaten by her Master. It was the most erotic, and satisfying, feeling I have ever had and from then on I welcomed each stroke as it helped turn me into the person I knew I really desired to be."

"I know!" Jenny replied wistfully. "I felt the same the first time Hassan took a whip to me."

"I heard he was very cruel to you. You must have loved him very much."

"I did," Jenny confessed. "He was the Master both I, and my body, needed. I even welcomed the degrading things he did to me, and made me do. The things the other girls at the Meetings hated so much."

Melanie, shocked at this last revelation, was spared from saying any more as Ayesha returned and the conversation ceased. She started to spread the cream over the damaged areas. Although she was as gentle as she could be, Melanie still could not suppress a few cries and moans as the woman's fingers touched the worst of the weals. The two women then helped Melanie to re-apply her make up and brush out her hair.

As the half hour allowed for her recovery drew to a close, Melanie made her way down to the lounge, where she fell to her knees before her Master. She raised her eyes to him and he smiled in satisfaction as he saw the utter submission, and adoration, as well as the pain that shone there. He was certain that, although her spirit had not been broken, she would still present him with ample opportunities in the future to chastise her in the manner they both enjoyed. His first application of a whip to her delicious body had been even more pleasing than he could have imagined. He silently berated himself for having waited so long before doing it.

CHAPTER 7.

That night, after her introduction to the whip, she was summoned to her Master's bed and the sex that followed surpassed anything that had gone before. Craig was both more masterful, yet tender with her bruised body, for which she was grateful, and she excelled herself in pleasuring him, including ways that, heretofore, she had never dreamed of performing.

The days that followed were idyllic and Melanie went about her duties with a self satisfied smile on her face. She was fully aware that the weals on her back and bottom from the whip were on full view and, secretly, she was proud of them. It seemed to her that Jenny was even friendlier than before, and Ayesha treated her with an element of respect that she had not shown until that evening.

Craig continued to attend the monthly Meetings but now he took both girls along with him. Paul had agreed and had arranged for one or two of his close friends, who had similar tastes but, at the time, no slave of their own, to attend and keep the numbers balanced. With Hassan no longer in attendance, Melanie and Jenny both came not only to enjoy these events, but to look forward to them. The other Masters and slaves who were there varied from month to month and this enhanced the novelty. Since whips were banned and only the girls' behinds were to be used as the target, the 'acts of submission' were well within their capability to endure without the element of fear becoming too overpowering to spoil the pleasure.

It was also nice to meet with other girls who were of a like mind, and Masters who so happily provided the pleasure they enjoyed. Craig was pleased with the compliments he received from the other Masters concerning both of his slaves. The teaching they had received from Ayesha had improved not only their deportment but also their prowess in pleasing their Masters for the weekends in bed at night. It was at the Meetings that Melanie found out that the threat to whip an unsatisfactory slave was no idle one.

It was one Sunday morning and Melanie had spent the night with a Master called Stephen. After her beating from him on the Saturday morning, which had been well within her capability to endure to his satisfaction, he had taken her to her room quite early on in the evening and the ensuing sex had been very enjoyable to both of them. He had, unusually for a temporary Master shown a lot of interest in her past and her time as Craig's slave. She had innocently answered his questions at the time without thought to the purpose behind them. This she was to find out some time later.

Instead of congregating in the lounge after breakfast, the Masters all followed Paul to his study. They were closeted there for over half an hour and, when they eventually emerged, went to the lounge and summoned the slaves to attend them there. The Masters were already seated along one wall and the slaves filed in, their eyes demurely downcast as Paul lined them up against another. It was only then that Melanie realised that the centre of the room had been cleared of furniture and that there was a thin chain hanging from a hook in the ceiling.

Paul rose to his feet and addressed the line of slaves.

"One of the Masters has complained that his 'slave for the Meeting' has not behaved satisfactorily during this weekend. The trial has taken place and the slave found guilty. The punishment agreed upon is fifteen lashes with a whip. The slave will also remain naked until the time comes to leave." Paul paused and looked hard at the

slaves, each one wondering if it was she that had been found at fault.

"Annette," Paul continued. "Step forward, strip and stand beneath the chain."

While the other slaves inwardly breathed a sigh of relief, Melanie happened to be looking at Annette as Paul made the announcement. The look of astonishment on the slave's face showed she had not even been expecting that it had been she that was at fault. Then the colour drained from her face as realisation sank in. She had been tried and condemned without being allowed to speak in her own defence. But, she was a slave and the Masters' word was law that must be accepted and obeyed without question. So she obeyed and stood, trembling under where the chain was suspended. Paul took her hands and clipped her wrist cuffs together. He raised her arms above her head, making her rise to her toes, and attached the cuffs to the end of the chain. He parted her long blonde hair and drew it forward over her breasts, baring her back for the lash.

The watching slaves could see Annette trembling with fear. Her pale skin on her buttocks was already marked and bruised from the 'introductory switching' she had received the previous morning. Peter, her Master, rose from his chair and collected the whip from a side table. He took up his position to his slave's rear and shook the lash lose. He raised his arm and, with a menacing hiss, sent the thong through the air. The lash curled across the top of Annette's back, making her gasp as the air was forced from her lungs and out through her clenched teeth.

Melanie shuddered as she watched the leather fall away, leaving a livid weal the full width of the slave's pale shoulders. Annette managed to take two more strokes before the first cry of pain echoed the report of the lash. As was the Masters' usual practice, Peter was applying the whip with sufficient force to cause terrible pain, but not hard enough to risk permanently marking the body of his slave.

As three more lashes were applied to Annette's back, her cries grew louder and she began to writhe as the leather curled around her sides and the flayed end of the thong sought out, and found, her tender breasts. Despite the natural urge to turn away from the source of her agony, Annette forced herself to keep her back towards her Master to avoid exposing the full areas of her breasts to the lash.

Melanie remembered back to her first attendance at a Meeting. Annette had, at that time, screamed early on during her introductory beating and how Melanie had wondered if she was not very experienced. But it had then been Hassan administering the beating and perhaps that was what made the girl appear less brave. Now, under the whip, she was demonstrating that she could withstand her punishment as well as any of the others.

As the fifth stroke added to the fire raging in her back, she let out the first full blooded scream. She continued to scream as the punishing thong bit into her back another four times. Peter paused and looked hard at his slave. Her legs had given way and her arms were taking all of her weight. The smooth whiteness of her back was well marked with livid raised weals that stretched the full width, some curling round her sides. He was making sure that she learned her lesson and would behave herself at future Meetings. Her bad behaviour was also a bad refection on him. With this thought in mind, he determined she would not forget the lesson. She still had six more lashes to come. So far, he had not overlapped any of the strokes and nine distinct weals, running almost parallel one to another, ran down her back.

The nine strokes had all been applied with a forehand motion and none had encroached on another. Now he changed to a backhand motion and the next three strokes all crossed the previous ones, making the slave's pain doubly worse. After the thirteenth stroke, he again paused for a moment or so to recover his breath and survey his slave's back. The last three strokes had made a pretty pattern diagonally over the previous nine.

He did not wish to risk marking her too severely so, taking careful aim, he brought the lash hissing through the air. To the astonishment of the spectators, the cruel thong cut into the cheeks of her buttocks, already made sore from the switching the previous day. He had decided, to avoid damaging her back further, to apply the last three strokes to her buttocks As the first of these bit into her flesh, Annette was taken by surprise and let out the loudest, pain racked, scream since her punishment had begun. Her body twisted causing the second stroke to cut into her unprotected sex. Her body jerked rigid as she let out a terrible scream. The final stroke mirrored the previous one and, as she absorbed the full agony her body again jerked rigid before collapsing but, this time as it relaxed, she descended into the blessed relief of unconsciousness. Her legs gave way and she hung suspended by her wrists.

All through the whipping, although she writhed frantically as the pain escalated, she had managed to keep her back towards her Master until the last strokes had cut into her buttocks. It was a lesson a slave learned early on. If she twisted and turned as the whip was laid on, the lash would seek out, and find, her breasts and sex. These most tender parts of their bodies received enough attention from their master's implements without subjecting them to lashes not intended for those areas.

Paul decreed that she must be left suspended for fifteen minutes to display her disgrace.

Watching the punishment administered, Melanie was thankful that Hassan no longer attended the Meetings, and that James had obviously not reported her that time when she had spoken out injudiciously when he said he thought of asking Craig to sell her to him. The thought of having to face a whipping, a terrible one no doubt as Craig would have taken it as a personal affront if she were ever found displeasing, with all the Masters and slaves watching was something she dared not think about. But at least, if that did happen, she had already been whipped by her Master in the privacy of his own house!

Fifteen minutes later, Annette, who had recovered consciousness but was still sobbing heavily with the pain, was released from the chain and collapsed in a heap on the floor, still shaking. Her back was a dreadful sight with livid raised weals standing out from her pale flesh. Her buttocks now had three heavier weals spread across them, each one with a thin line of bright red along its centre where the skin had been cut. Yasmin helped her to her feet. Annette turned to face the Masters and apologised for having been displeasing and thanked her Master for her whipping. Yasmin and another girl, took her upstairs to the bathroom where, before returning her to the lounge, they bathed her and repaired her appearance. As was ordained, she remained naked for the remainder of the morning until Peter ordered her to dress, preparatory to leaving.

It was during the period between Annette's whipping and their departure, that Melanie noticed Craig was in deep, earnest conversation with Stephen. Stephen was one of the unattached Masters Paul introduced each time she and Jenny were taken to the Meetings and Melanie had been drawn as his slave for the weekend. He had proved a natural Master, both when she reported to him in the Dungeon to receive twenty strokes of the cane across her bottom and, later, when she had submitted to him for the night.

Part of Melanie's mind went back to the previous evening. Normally, Masters did not talk to their 'slave' on matters concerning the beatings they received from their true Masters. But, on this occasion, Stephen had asked her whether she and Jenny had been whipped, details of the type of whips that had been used on them, the number of lashes they could take and how well they had taken them. Despite the unusualness of the questioning, Melanie had replied giving him all the details he asked for. He had seemed very pleased with her responses.

Now, as she went about her duties of serving the Masters, Melanie saw the two men talking and, as they did so, occasionally giving her and Jenny careful glances. She wondered what they were discussing but was unable to think of anything which would involve them studying herself and Jenny so intently.

On the journey home, Craig was silent and, clearly, in deep thought. He had ordered the two slaves to remain silent so as not to disturb him so Melanie's curiosity had to remain unanswered. It was not until three days later that she was to become aware of the discussion between the two men and the reason for their studied glances towards Jenny and herself. The two slaves were summoned to attend their Master in his study. Having entered, they sank to their knees, already aware of Ayesha's presence. Both wondered for what reason they had been summoned. Had they given cause for their Master to be displeased with them? Would his next order be for them to report to the Correction Room for a thrashing?

"At the Meeting last weekend," Craig broke the silence. "I had an offer from one of the Masters to purchase both of you."

At his words, Melanie felt the colour drain from her face and her legs began to shake.

Had he accepted the offer? Was she already sold to another? Was her world to come to an end?

"Stephen Malanski, the Master who enjoyed your pleasures Melanie, is a film director and he is having considerable difficulty with his latest film. The story line partly involves the transportation of criminals to the colonies. During the voyage, two of the female prisoners cause a riot in the hold and have to be punished with a flogging. One of them is the heroine of the story and he has tried several ways to film the scene but, being a perfectionist, he has not been able to make the finished effect believable. Neither the efforts of the Make Up department, nor the offer of a high bonus to any body double he could find, have worked."

Craig paused in his monologue to study both slaves intently. He had seen the brief look of horror swiftly pass across Melanie's face as she had heard of Stephen's offer and was satisfied. If she thought that being sold was the only alternative, she would more readily accept the situation he was about to thrust upon them. Even if Jenny was reluctant, Melanie would soon persuade her to go along with the idea.

"Since you, Melanie, closely resemble the leading lady, he wanted to buy you both and have the whipping carried out for real. Since he had no intention of keeping you afterwards, he made the mistake of informing me that he would probably sell you on to a brothel."

Melanie and Jenny had listened as Craig continued his oration with mounting dread. Neither wished to end up in any sort of brothel. Melanie because she had determined to spend the rest of her life as Craig's slave and Jenny because, having got over losing Hassan as her Master, had accepted her present situation as the best alternative.

"However," Craig continued. "I had no intention of selling either of you, so I refused his very handsome offer. But, to help him out of his problem, I agreed that he could use you both for the scene provided that I applied the flogging and used one of my own whips. We discussed this possibility for some time and he accepted my offer, insisting that I be well recompensed financially for my time and his use of you."

Again, Craig paused. Both slaves had, inwardly breathed a sigh of relief at the news that they were not, after all to be sold, but their joy was tempered by the knowledge that they would, instead, have to endure a whipping that would not only be incorporated in a film which thousands of strangers would see, but that there would be the film crew, and probably many other spectators to witness the event. How many people would, in the future, recognise them?

Almost divining their thoughts, Craig continued. "Stephen has assured me that the make-up people would ensure that you would not be recognisable to anyone who might meet you in the future. The filming will take place as soon as your bodies are free from any signs of punishment. In the meantime, since I will have to refrain from beating you, any offences which you may commit will be recorded and punishment meted out at a later date. You may go, now, and resume your duties."

As soon as they had departed from the room, Jenny turned to Melanie and began to remonstrate with her about what, to all intents and purposes, was nothing less than a public whipping before a crowd of strangers. That they would not be recognisable as themselves to anyone viewing the film at a later date was, to her way of thinking, no consolation.

During the next day or so, when the slaves were alone, the matter continued to be debated between them, Melanie desperately trying to convince Jenny to go along with their Master's plan. Slowly but surely, she managed to convince her sister slave that submitting willingly to the flogging was the only alternative to displeasing their Master and incurring his intense anger. Anger, as Melanie pointed out, that might well result in him disposing of them in a manner that would be too terrible to contemplate!

Jenny, for her part being loath to be passed on to some unknown master and whatever fate he might have in store for her, finally agreed to play her part. At least, as she admitted, the whipping would be over and done with quickly and not only would they please their Master but would, hopefully secure their future with him.

In order to protect their identity as much as possible, Stephen visited Craig's house on several occasions and coached the girls in the parts they would have to act. They were both quick learners and were soon word perfect in the few instances where they would be required to speak and in the manner they would have to conduct themselves when on set. The one thing that ran contrary to their nature was that they were not, under any circumstances, to endure the whippings with the fortitude they usually displayed when under punishment. Whilst the characters they would be playing were hardened criminals, they were not accustomed to being flogged and they must react to the pain accordingly. Stephen was emphatic that they understood their parts, and would act correctly for, as he explained, there would be only the one opportunity to film the scenes.

During the days that followed, Craig lost no opportunity in going over the proposed scenes with them. He emphasised that he would be the person applying the whip and he would ensure that, whilst the marks must be utterly convincing, there was no danger of them being permanently scarred. Stephen had pointed out that the script called for the ship's captain to order the punishments, it also required that the 'bosun', in this case Craig, would be ordered to administer the flogging with sufficient force to punish them for their offence but not scar the prisoners' bodies and so reduce their saleable value at the end of the voyage. Both girls received this news thankfully. They were both aware that, in the times in which the film was set, shipboard floggings were notorious for their savagery and the permanent damage done to the unfortunate recipient.

The days that followed were a trial for the slaves. Each day, Craig closely inspected their bodies to assess the degree of their recovery. Ayesha applied the special cream three times a day and, at the end of a week, Craig judged that their skin was sufficiently clear for Stephen's satisfaction. In fact, both of their bodies showed no signs of having been beaten. He immediately phoned Stephen and arranged to take the girls to the film studio on the following Wednesday. As he was in a good mood, he did not hesitate to point out, it would be an appropriate 'present' for Melanie since that day was her twenty fourth birthday.

Having made an early start, taking Ayesha with them, they duly arrived at their destination at nine thirty in the morning. Following Stephen's instructions, Craig had made for a door at the rear of the huge building which housed the set to be used. Stephen met them at the door and gave each slave a dark hooded cloak to put on. Avoiding meeting any other person, he hustled them to Make Up, leaving Ayesha in a side room on the way. Here, three assistants, who had been sworn to secrecy, began preparing the slaves and Craig for their performance. Both Melanie and Jenny were horrified at the manner they were prepared. Their faces, arms and legs were dirtied and their hair rubbed with grease and dirt.

The assistants took great care over the preparations and, when they had finally finished, both girls, viewing themselves in mirrors, could hardly believe their eyes. Even to themselves, they had to admit they bore little or no resemblance to the two girls that had entered the building. The chances of anyone, viewing the film, recognising them were almost nil. In the meantime, Crag had also submitted to the assistants' attention and likewise, was not recognisable. Finally, he was dressed in his sailor's uniform and the two girls, having been ordered to strip naked, were given a thin, ragged shift to wear.

Stephen arrived at this stage and conducted all three to the other room, to which Ayesha had already been conducted. Looking round, the girls saw that two divan beds had been put in there and Ayesha had laid out on a small table her jar of cream together with a bowl of cold water and cloths. Stephen made them repeat the instructions he and Craig had been drumming into them on the parts they were to play. By this time, both girls were nervous and anxious to get the business over with as soon as possible. Fortunately, Stephen had anticipated this and informed them that all was ready for the 'shooting' to take place. He led them from the room to the entrance to the 'set' and introduced them to the four men, dressed as sailors, who would escort them to the whipping place.

Some three minutes later, a voice called, 'bring forth the prisoners' and, with a man on each side grasping their arms, they girls were led onto the set. Momentarily dazzled by the bright lighting, Melanie blinked several times and then stared round with astonishment. To all intents and purposes, they had been led onto the well deck of a sailing ship. But for the absence of motion, she could well believe they were actually on board ship. But for the cause of her presence there it would have been an exciting and educating experience seeing how the films she had watched in the cinema and on television had been made. Then her eyes caught sight of a large grating that had been placed against one side of the deck and lashed securely to the rigging that ascended to the high ceiling above. This was clearly where they would be put to be flogged and she felt her legs begin to shake with fear. Stephen called for silence, then for the cameras to roll.

"The two prisoners, Ann Smith and Jane Fisher are guilty of causing a riot." The loud and stern voice of the 'ship's captain' echoed round the set. "I will not tolerate such behaviour on my ship. Let the punishment that is to be

152

meted out to these two be a warning to any others who may be tempted to follow their example. They are each sentenced to twenty lashes."

A gasp of astonishment came from the crowd of extras who were acting as the ship's company and the other prisoners, who had been brought on deck to witness the punishment. The gasp was repeated as they watched 'Mr Bosun' take a cat-o-nine tails from the bag he was holding in his hand. Their horror would have been even more when they found out that the whipping was to be for real and not merely acting.

"Mr Bosun," the captain continued. "You may begin with Jane Fisher."

Immediately, the two men holding Jenny moved to lead her to the grating. Playing her part as ordered, Jenny began to struggle violently and yelled curses at the captain, and the men holding her. But the men were ready for this and dragged her, still yelling, to the grating. One pulled her arms above her head as the other, grasping the hem of her shift, dragged it up over head and threw it to one side. Each grasping a wrist, they pulled her arms up and outwards and tied her wrists to the corners of the grating. Her ankles were forced apart and dealt with in the same manner. Finally, they pulled her hair to one side, so that her face was towards one of the cameras and tied it to the grating.

Melanie, knowing her turn was still to come, watched in apprehension as Craig, shaking loose the thongs of the 'cat' took up his position and the First Mate stood to one side, ready to count the strokes out loud.

"Mr Bosun." The captain's voice broke the silence that had descended on the set. "The prisoner needs to be taught a lesson in manners. In view of the outburst we have just witnessed, you will increase the sentence to twenty-five lashes."

"Aye, Aye, Sir!" Craig acknowledged the order.

Melanie watched in apprehension as Craig raised the whip and sent the thongs whistling through the air to land with a resounding 'crack' across Jenny's bare back.

"Bastard! I'll kill you for this!" Jenny yelled, nearly drowning the sound of the count, as her body was thrown against the grating by the force of the stroke.

She screamed in pain and continued to yell curses as three more strokes lashed across her back. Then, as the fifth cut into her, she had no breath for curses and could only scream as the agony in her back escalated.

Melanie tore her eyes away from the sight of her friend spread against the grating her back already bearing the signs of the whipping. She looked, instead, at the group of people, those acting as the prisoners, who had been brought up from below decks to witness the punishment. Clearly, they had not been forewarned that what was to happen would be for real, not playacting. The expressions on their faces ranged from utter horror to complete disbelief. There was no doubt in their minds that the girl lashed to the grating was, in deed, being properly whipped. The faces of a few, those more upset than the others, had turned a ghastly green colour. The men, acting as the crew of the ship were equally stunned by the spectacle they were watching.

Melanie turned her head back to look again at Jenny. The girl's back was, by now, well marked with cruel, livid, weals that stretching from the top of her shoulders down to her waist. She was still screaming and writhing as the leathers ploughed onto her back and Melanie was shaken as she heard that the count had only reached twelve. Her sister slave still had another thirteen lashes to come! Then it would be her turn. She made up her mind that, not only would she submit meekly and not create a scene as Jenny had done, but she would 'put on a show'. Stephen had previously ordered that Jenny would 'play up' and that Melanie would not. Jenny had played her part well, not realising that, in doing so, she had earned herself five extra lashes.

By the time the count had reached seventeen, Jenny had ceased screaming and writhing and her body hung suspended by her wrists, her legs no longer being able to support her weight. The only reaction to the thongs thudding onto her back was a sharp jerk as her body was thrown against the grating with each stroke. That she was still conscious was evidenced by the moaning and mewing that emanated from her throat.

At last, the thongs lashed her back for the final stroke and the First Mate called out 'twenty-five' and a sigh of relief issued from the watchers. For a moment or two Jenny hung there, her body wringing with sweat, caused both by the heat of the stage lighting and her ordeal.

"Cut her down and take her to the sick bay!" the captain ordered.

Two crew members hurried to obey and, as gently as they could, released Jenny's bonds and, before she could slide down onto the deck, eased her, face down, onto a plank and carried her off the set.

"Mr Bosun!" the Captain called out. "Proceed with the punishment of Ann Smith."

Melanie had been apprehensively awaiting this order to be given. Carrying out her determination to 'give them a show' she wrenched herself free from the grasp of the two men who held her and began to walk slowly towards the grating. As she did so, she reached down, grasped the hem of her shift and pulled it off over her head, throwing it to one side. She had caught the men by surprise and, by the time they had recovered, she had reached the grating and spread eagled her body against it. She turned her head towards the group of 'prisoners' and gave them a broad smile. The two men, recovered from the shock of her display, tied her wrists and ankles to the grating and turning her head towards the same camera that Jenny had faced, pulled her hair up above her had and tied it to the grating. They then stood to one side.

The Captain called out; "Twenty lashes, please, and lay them on hard."

Melanie had clearly not behaved in any way to earn extra, as Jenny had done, but Stephen was annoyed at her display of arrogance and had decided to reward her accordingly.

"Aye, Aye, Sir!" Craig responded, as he again resumed his position.

Melanie clamped her fists tight onto the grating and clenched her teeth, preparing herself for the ordeal to come. Having already seen the force her Master had used in flogging Jenny, she knew he had laid the whip on with almost full strength and she had no illusions about the way he would deal with her.

Those watching had been astounded by the apparently submissive way she had

prepared herself. They knew she had seen the other girl severely whipped and that she was in for the same ordeal. They were even more stunned as she took four lashes before the first sounds erupted from her throat. She had made up her mind to take more than that in silence but Craig was laying on the whip harder than he had ever done before. As the count passed through five to nine, her cries grew louder and, as the tenth lashed her pain-filled back, she threw back her head as far as the bonds in her hair would allow and screamed. Through the haze of pain, she felt the sweat running down her body. She managed to keep her grip fastened on the struts of the grating as the thongs continued to add to the furnace burning in her back.

Now all those watching were staring in utter disbelief at the scene they were witnessing. It was beyond their comprehension that any woman would agree to be flogged at all, let alone in public. Jenny's struggles and verbal abuse, they had thought were because she had been, somehow, forced into submitting to the ordeal. But that Melanie had gone to her fate so calmly and, apparently willingly, had stunned them completely. That she had endured four strokes in silence and not screamed until the thongs had cut into her back for the tenth stroke was astonishing.

Due to her screaming, and the pain ravaging her back, Melanie had not heard the count being called after the tenth stroke so, when her legs finally failed to support her weight, she had no idea that she only had four more strokes to come. These she received in silence except for a loud moaning and mewing, which increased in volume each time the thongs cut into her back and she absorbed the agony of the remaining lashes of her punishment.

"Cut her down and take her below," the Captain ordered. "And return the prisoners to the hold."

As carefully as Jenny had been handled, Melanie was released, laid on a plank and carried from the set. She was hazily aware of being carried to the room where they had waited before going onto the set and of being gently lifted and placed, face down, on the divan. Immediately, Ayesha got to work on her back with the cream. Slowly, Melanie returned to full consciousness and, turning her head to one side, saw Jenny lying on the other divan, still sobbing quietly as waves of pain continued to flow through her body.

Craig, having had the make up removed and again dressed as before, entered the room. Making no comment, he inspected his two slaves and had a whispered conversation with Ayesha. They were obviously in no condition to move yet and he instructed Ayesha to remain with them, give them cold drinks to help their recovery and lock the door after he had passed through and only open it to his summons. Two hours later he returned with Stephen and ordered Ayesha to prepare the slaves for departure. The concealing cloak was put over each of them and with Stephen leading to ensure the way back to the car was free from any observation, they were ushered to the car and ordered into the back seat.

The journey home was a terrible ordeal for the slaves. The slightest fault in the road surface causing the car to bump or jerk, sent renewed waves of pain through their bodies. They were grateful when they arrived home and Craig ordered Ayesha to take the slaves to their rooms and let them rest for a few hours before resuming their duties. Melanie relaxed in the comfort of her own bed and happily recalled the day as being her best birthday ever.

The slaves' bodies quickly recovered from their ordeal, thanks to the care and attention Ayesha expended on them for that purpose. Their minds were not to recover so quickly. Stephen sent Craig a copy of the scenes in which they featured and he watched them over and over again. He made the slaves kneel at his side and, at first, they shuddered and jerked as each stroke was applied. But, after they had seen the showings several times, they watched with detached enthusiasm.

The film was released soon afterwards and Stephen received considerable applause as the scenes in which the two prisoners were whipped were discussed. Without divulging their identities, Stephen astounded some of the other producers and directors when he informed them that the whippings were for real and not merely tricks of the trade as were employed in that class of film. S & M erotic films, or other films were an element of such cruelty was involved were becoming more popular and the audiences more critical. It was becoming increasingly difficult for the make up departments and the cutting editors to ensure their tastes were adequately catered for. Stephen received so many demands for the girls to be made available to these producers, that he eventually agreed to approach

Craig to test out the ground for further use of his slaves.

Craig was reluctant to entertain any such proposal at first but Stephen persisted, pointing out that considerable financial incentives would be put his way. Eventually, Craig agreed to consider any offer but only on the same conditions that had prevailed for Stephen's film; that the girls were made unrecognisable and that no whips were used, unless he provided them and applied the whippings, and that the beatings were not too sadistic.

Consequently, over the next four or five years, Melanie and Jenny found themselves

acting the parts of senior school girls, maids, secretaries, errant wives and girlfriends and numerous other characters. The beatings they received were well within their capacity to endure, but they sometimes found it taxing to act as if it were the first time they were thrashed. As each film was released to the public, Craig received a copy and these were added to his collection. His, and the girls, identities' were so well guarded that not even the slaves and Masters at the monthly Meetings knew it was Melanie and Jenny acting the parts.

CHAPTER 8.

Life in Craig's household was idyllic for Melanie. She revelled in her submission and even having to share her Master with Jenny, and even Ayesha's presence in the house did nothing to mar her happiness.

Ayesha had, by this time, taught them to perform the dances of her country and both slaves had become very proficient. Craig had kept a close watch on their progress and, as soon as Ayesha informed him of their ability, had them entertain him in the lounge of an evening. Watching their near naked bodies seductively turning and twisting before him always aroused him and he made it a finale to the evening to take them both to bed.

Both slaves had, by now, become very proficient with their dancing and Melanie, especially, revelled in the lusting looks that Craig gave her each time she performed for him. Not even the incident that occurred one morning not long after her whipping at the film studio, as she was helping to prepare the lunch detracted from her happiness, although it was very demeaning

She was helping in the kitchen as part of her duties for the day. Due to her euphoric state, she was not concentrating on what was happening around her. She turned to reach for a drying cloth and bumped into Ayesha. She was about to apologise when she saw that she had knocked a dish that the woman was carrying and that the contents, some gravy, had spilled on the floor.

"Why don't you concentrate on what you're doing, you clumsy wench!" The woman exploded. "I will not have you going about in a day dream in my kitchen. You need teaching a lesson. Bare your behind and bend over the end of the table."

Melanie, aghast that she was to be beaten by the woman for the first time, quickly bent over the table and pulled her shift up well over her back. She watched Ayesha take down the strap from the hook where it was kept and move behind her.

Melanie was conscious that her buttocks had not yet fully recovered from a caning she had received a few days earlier and braced herself. The strap lashed across her bottom with a force that she had certainly not expected. She had not expected that a woman, even one as well built as Ayesha, could lay a strap on with such force. A line of pain erupted in her cheeks making her jerk forward and a stifled groan escaped her open mouth. This was quickly followed by five more strokes that set her buttocks on fire and it was all she could do to keep from crying out. When she was ordered to get up, her hands flew to the injured area. She was amazed how hot it felt. From then on she concentrated on what she was doing. Whilst she delighted in being beaten by her Master, or another man for that matter, to have to bend, bare her behind and be beaten by a woman was just too humiliating; it was an experience she vowed to avoid having to repeat. If Ayesha reported the incident to Craig, as she was supposed to do, her Master refrained from commenting on it. To her relief! Either the woman had not reported the incident or, more likely, her Master chose to ignore it, leaving the matter in Ayesha's hands.

A second incident occurred some three days after the last marks on the slaves' bodies had disappeared, which was to have a profound effect on her existence. She was coming out of the kitchen one morning when her Master ordered her to follow him to the Correction Room and stand behind the Judgement Seat. As he sat down in front of her she wondered what offence Jenny had committed this time. There was a knock on the door and, in response to Craig's command Jenny entered and sank to her knees in front of her Master.

"Slave, you were late in rising this morning and,

consequently failed to carry out your duties, and have been summoned for punishment. Because of your failure, Melanie had to bring me my early morning tea."

So that was it, Melanie thought. She had arrived early in the kitchen that morning to find Ayesha in an angry state. She pointed to a tray on the table and ordered her to take it up to the Master quickly. Melanie, thinking it was her turn complied hastily and, since no more had been said on the matter, had completely forgotten it. It was only on hearing the charge against her sister slave that she remembered that it had been Jenny's turn that morning.

"You are to be thrashed with the cane across your buttocks," she heard Craig pronounce. The routine for a punishment followed its usual course until Jenny was secured over the bars, her bare buttocks quivering in anticipation of the flogging to come.

Craig picked up the cane and, instead of taking his position alongside the bent slave, approached Melanie, holding the cane out to her.

"Since it was you who had to do the slave's work, you will administer her beating." He said.

Melanie looked at him in horror. "I couldn't do that, Master!" she said.

"You can, and will," Craig retorted. "You will give her twenty five stokes, as I have ordered. You will lay them on hard and make her scream. If I think you are holding back, you will take her place and get fifty with the switch across your back. Now do as I ordered."

Reluctantly, Melanie took the cane and walked towards the bent slave. She halted and laid the cane against Jenny's bottom, shuffling her feet to get the best stance. She heard Craig ask the usual questions and Jenny's responses.

"Proceed with the punishment," Craig ordered.

Melanie had never beaten anyone before and was not certain how to go about it, but she remembered watching

162

how her Master had beaten Jenny on previous occasions. She raised the cane and brought it down across Jenny's behind. A dull report sounded in the room.

"Harder!" Craig's loud shout made her jump. "Remember what I said. I want to hear you make her scream. If you do not do it properly, you will be soundly switched."

Again, Melanie laid the cane across the proffered buttocks. This time a gasp echoed the report as Jenny began to feel the greater effort Melanie had now put behind the stroke. Time and time again Melanie's arm rose and fell as she beat her friend's behind. As she got into the rhythm, she found that two things were happening. Firstly Jenny was beginning to cry out, witnessing that the strokes were increasing in force. Out of the corner of her eye, she saw a smile appear on Craig's face as the colour of Jenny's cheeks changed from a milky whiteness to red, and distinct lines of darker red showed where the more forceful strokes were falling.

The second thing that occurred to Melanie was that she was rapidly becoming aroused as the beating progressed. She was already aware that watching another being beaten had aroused her but, being the first time she had wielded the rod, she was disturbed to see that her body reacted in the same way but even more so. She realised she was enjoying what she was doing! This, and the arousal, had the effect of giving more power to her arm and soon Jenny was yelling out loud. Then the yells turned to pain racked screams.

"Enough!" Craig commanded as he watched the cane impact with Jenny's buttocks for the twenty fifth stroke.

Melanie ceased the thrashing. For the first time since she had begun, she looked carefully at Jenny's buttocks and was horrified at the damage she had inflicted there. Her own arousal was forgotten as she rushed round in front of the heavily sobbing girl and fell to her knees. She reached her hands to the tear sodden face and started to stroke away the tears, at the same time cooing that she was sorry and begging her friend to forgive her.

Craig soon put a stop to this display, ordered Melanie to release the slave and return to her place behind the Judgement Seat. The punishment routine then progressed to the closing stage when Jenny thanked her Master, and the cane, for her beating. Then to Melanie's horror, Jenny looked up at her and, with a smile on her face, also thanked her for caning her. Jenny rose and exited the room. Craig ordered Melanie to continue with her duties.

Some time later, the two girls were alone in the kitchen. Melanie, still feeling guilty for what she had done, and more so for having enjoyed doing it, apologised to her friend and, again begged her forgiveness.

"There is nothing to forgive!" Jenny interrupted her. "I liked being beaten by you, so don't feel guilty. It is something I have wanted to happen for some time now."

Melanie was flabbergasted! "You have wanted me to do that to you! I don't understand. Why?"

"Why? Because I love you," Jenny replied to Melanie's further amazement. "I fell in love with you when I saw you at that first Meeting you attended. But don't let our Master know, whatever you do, or we may both be whipped. I just hope that you enjoyed doing it as much as I did being on the receiving end."

Melanie was stunned by this revelation. She thought about it for some days and the more she thought the more she came to not only accept what Jenny had said but realised she had similar feelings about her sister slave. That her body had been aroused as she had lashed the cane across her friend's bare buttocks, she kept to herself. It seemed natural, after a day or so when they found themselves alone and unlikely to be discovered, that the two girls began to fondle and kiss each other. Melanie, who had in the past, lain abed and masturbated herself to a climax, found it both intriguing and a pleasure to slip her fingers between Jenny's sex lips and deep into her tunnel and listen to the gasps and sighs of satisfaction issue from the other girl. Likewise she discovered deep enjoyment when Jenny insisted in pleasuring her in return.

Several months passed after that day when Melanie caned Jenny's bottom. During those the sexual relationship between the two slaves flourished. They had to be ultra careful as to be discovered by either Ayesha or their Master would have led to consequences neither dared contemplate.

Unbeknown to either girl, Craig had noticed how Melanie had been aroused as she administered the thrashing, and the smile on Jenny's face as she thanked her afterwards. At first he had been taken aback by this but, on reflection, it provided him with a certain pleasure. As a consequence, occasionally, when neither of the slaves had transgressed, he summoned them to the Punishment Room and had them cane, or switch, each other for his amusement. Little did he realise just how much pleasure, perhaps of a different sort, his slaves derived from these times. Neither did he realise how the relationship between them had changed. Melanie, to her surprise, soon found that being beaten by Jenny was also enjoyable, unlike the times when Ayesha took the strap to her.

The slaves' behaviour each time he had them cane or switch, each other kept recurring in Craig's mind. Eventually the truth dawned on him. That they were both displaying lesbian tendencies came as a shock. They had both shown such distinctly heterosexual responses whenever he took them to bed, or enjoyed them as they lay tied over the bars after a thrashing, that any other sexual inclinations had not crossed his mind. But then he remembered seeing the strange glances the slaves cast at each other when they thought they were not being watched.

At first he was horrified and contemplated warning them that it had to stop or he would sell them to a brothel. But he hesitated to take this course of action. He derived too much pleasure from their educated bodies and he did not want to deprive himself of that. As his mind dwelt on the problem, he had an idea. Why not use this discovery to his advantage? It would be a novel experience to watch them entertaining him, and his guests, in this fashion. It would add another source of entertainment to their dancing.

One evening, he summoned his two slaves to the lounge. He ordered them to strip and play with each other. At first the girls displayed horror, whether at this order or the fear that their secret had been discovered, he was not sure.

"I am fully aware that you both enjoy such pleasures. Now, obey my order and do it properly. Just as you would if I were not watching."

Melanie and Jenny exchanged puzzled glances, wondering how he had discovered their secret.

"Get on with it, unless you both want a thrashing!" Craig shouted, annoyed at their delay in obeying.

Slowly the two girls shed their costumes and sank to the floor. Trying to hide their embarrassment at having him see them in action, and concern that their secret had been discovered, they began to fondle each other. Soon the desires that flowed through them overcame their reservations and they became carried away.

Craig watched fascinated at the display. As his slaves became immersed in their passion, they clearly forgot his presence and soon gasps, and moans, of pleasure echoed round the room. Their bodies began to glow with sweat and he could clearly see their juices flowing from their sexes. Loud squelching sounds came from them as the other's fingers delved deep inside the tunnel. Far from being disgusted, as he had first thought he would be, he was amused and enjoyed the display and was soon shouting encouragement to them as he saw their climaxes approaching. Both came at the same time with screams of release as their orgasms shuddered through their bodies until, with a final yell of satisfaction, they collapsed on the carpet.

Craig continued to sit, staring at the prone slaves, who lay as if unconscious before him. It had been both a fascinating and, to his surprise, entertaining episode. One that, he decided, would be repeated at suitable intervals. The slaves' bodies were drenched in sweat and he could see the trails seeping down their thighs where their juices had been expelled. Slowly the slaves returned to awareness and he smiled to himself as he saw their faces redden with embarrassment as they realised what they had been made to do.

"Kneel, slaves," he commanded.

Melanie and Jenny obeyed, keeping their eyes fixed on the carpet in front of them.

"That was very educating," Craig continued. "I had intended to forbid you to continue with this aspect of your relationship but have decided not to. You may make love to each other in the privacy of your rooms, provided it does not interfere with your duties or distract from your duty to serve and please me. I will require you to repeat the performance at intervals for my entertainment and, when appropriate, in front of any guests that I may think would enjoy the experience."

A gasp from both slaves interrupted his discourse. The relief at not being severely flogged on the discovery of their secret had turned to dismay at his announcement. They would have to do it in front of his guests! Maybe at one of the monthly Meetings!

"Now, go and clean yourselves and continue with your duties," Craig ordered.

Both slaves left the lounge and made their way upstairs.

Neither spoke until they gained the washroom adjoining Melanie's room

"He wouldn't make us do that in front of his friends, would he?" Jenny asked.

"He said he would," Melanie replied. "He does not make threats, or promises, that he does not intend keeping. You ought to be well aware of that by now."

"But that would be awful," Jenny whispered. "I don't think I could do it. I love you but I wouldn't want our love to be the subject of amusement."

"Well if the time does come, you'll just have to, or we both could be severely whipped. He might even let the disappointed guests whip us," Melanie answered.

Jenny stayed silent after that. She remembered watching Annette whipped at the Meeting and how embarrassed the girl had been. It was something that both slaves had vowed would never happen to them. But would it? What if one of the Masters made false accusations against them? They were not allowed to speak in their own defence – just submit willingly to the inevitable! Now that Hassan was no longer a member of the group, the likelihood of that occurring was remote. Or so they hoped!

Whenever neither was summoned to their Master's bed at night, the two slaves made the best of his licence and indulged themselves in each others' bodies. But they had to also ensure they had a good night's rest afterwards as they dared not be negligent in their duties the next day. When one had been beaten, the other always insisted that she spent the entire time at their disposal in pleasuring the other and soothing the bruises on her body.

Craig got so much enjoyment in their displays, both dancing and sexual, that it was not long before he ordered them to perform at the Meetings. With the threat of a public whipping hanging over their heads, both slaves did their best and soon overcame any embarrassment they felt. The dancing was no problem. Both enjoyed performing and revelled in the praise that their efforts received. The Masters maintained that it added an extra spice to the weekends, especially when one, or both, of the slaves performed the 'Veil' or 'Whip' dance.

The one dance that always brought extra applause was the 'Whip' dance. In this, a slave, who performed solo, danced as if she were being flogged with a whip. To make it even more realistic, Craig, having practiced in the secrecy of his home, took part, cracking a whip within inches of the slave's gyrating body. After several miss hits in practice, he had become proficient with the whip and, at the end of the dance, the slave had no marks on her body. Melanie liked this dance most of all. She felt she was publicly displaying her total submission to her Master.

Melanie had, whilst enjoying a few minutes free from the demands of the Masters at the monthly Meetings, found that Paul had quite a collection of books and magazines about the subject of modern day slavery, mainly relating to the type imposed on the slaves who attended the Meetings. She had perused these with interest, although there were certain things she read about that were foreign to her. Mention was made of needles, clamps and waxing that left her bemused as the reading matter gave no explanation of what was meant by these things or for what purpose they might be employed in the context of the magazine in which she read about them. It was part of her education that was lacking and which was shortly to be corrected.

Craig had taken her and Jenny to a Meeting and, after they had settled in and everyone had arrived, the Masters and slaves congregated in the lounge as usual to determine who would serve who for the weekend. It was only as she looked round that Melanie discovered that, instead of the six couples that always made up the quorum, there were in fact seven couples present. The explanation soon followed as Paul addressed the gathering.

"You will no doubt have realised that, this month, there are seven Masters and their slaves present. This is because neither Yasmin nor I, are to take part in the draw or the usual act of submission this morning. The reason for this will be explained this afternoon."

When he had finished, the draw took place, the remaining slaves made their submission to their temporary Master, Melanie and Jenny receiving sixteen strokes of the switch and eighteen strokes of the birch respectively, and the day continued as usual until after lunch. The slaves who had made their submission were, as usual, naked displaying their thrashed buttocks but Yasmin, alone, continued to wear her costume. The slaves were curious, and a little apprehensive, about Paul's announcement but not even Yasmin, who denied all knowledge of his plans, could enlighten them. Paul had been absent for some time during the morning and had made no explanation for his absence.

An hour after lunch, he requested that the Masters join him in the Dungeon and bring their slaves with them. On arriving there, they found that seating had been arranged along one wall and the Masters were asked to take their seats there, with their naked slaves for the weekend kneeling at their sides.

"Whilst we all appreciate Melanie and Jenny entertaining us with their dancing, I have thought of another way to liven up our Meetings." Paul broke the silence that had descended upon the room. "Subject to the approval of the Masters, I would like to instigate a competition between the slaves. This will take the form of an endurance test, the details of which I will explain in a moment. From now on, the complement at the Meetings will be increased to seven. Each month, a slave, who has not previously taken the test, will be randomly selected before the draw and she, and her temporary Master will take no further part in the draw and, consequently the slave will not perform her submission in the morning."

He paused and looked round and was pleased to see that his audience were listening to him attentively. They had, so far, displayed no antagonism to his suggestion although a degree of apprehension could be seen on the faces of the slaves. He reached behind him to where a large clipboard stood on an easel.

"Each slave's results will be displayed on this board in the form of a table, with the one who displays the highest stamina at the top and the others in descending order. Once all the slaves have taken the test once, it will be open to competition for any true Master to challenge for his slave to attempt to climb the ladder by retaking the test and trying o improve on her previous performance. I must insist that the true Masters promise that, as this competition is for our entertainment, no slave will suffer punitive measures on returning home if their standing in the table is not to their Master's satisfaction. Before a decision is made as to whether the competition is adopted as a part of the standard schedule of events for each Meeting, I will give a demonstration of the form the competition will take. Then the Masters can decide whether it will become a regular part of the proceedings. I must stress that Yasmin has no idea of the form the demonstration is to take and, therefore has not been able to prepare herself."

He then ordered Yasmin to strip and stand in the whipping frame. He secured her wrists and ankles to the corners as if for a flogging but allowed a certain amount of slackness in the securing chains. The seating had been so placed that the Masters, and the slaves kneeling beside them, had a sideways view of the displayed slave.

"First," Paul began to explain. "Nipple and labia clamps will be attached so."

He proceeded to do this, making Yasmin gasp as each clamp bit into her tender flesh. He then attached one end of a length of wire to each clamp and the other end to rings in the wall facing the slave, pulling the wires until they stretched taut. Then he went to the end of the room and returned with three candle sticks, each with a thick candle inserted, and placed these in front of Yasmin, just a few inches away from her body. Two were tall enough that the top of the candles were level with her breasts and the third level with her sex lips. Before attaching the clamps to his slave's body, he had held them up so that the other slaves and Masters could see them clearly. Melanie shuddered as she saw that each clamp was armed with a row of tiny sharp teeth that, she realised, would bite terribly into tender flesh.

"When the competition is to start," Paul continued to explain. "The candles will be lit. The slave's Weekend Master will proceed to thrash the slave with a tawse across her back and buttocks, applying the strokes alternately to each area. Clearly, if the slave flinches forward, she will risk scorching her breasts, or, if she pulls back, the clamps will inflict pain in her breasts and sex. The slave's power of endurance will be judged by how many strokes she can take before she dislodges one or more of the clamps from her body."

Paul paused and looked round his audience. The Masters were smiling, clearly thinking of the entertainment this would provide, but the slaves' faces were not so receptive. The pain they would have to endure was, to be sure, well appreciated. To have to remain rigid, not moving back or forward, as they were lashed would be difficult, not only because of the pain but the force of the impact of the tawse on their bodies would make keeping still even more difficult. As a test of stamina and endurance, it would surely, be a hard one.

"Are there any questions?" Paul asked.

The Masters, who had fully understood the severity of the test and were assessing the capabilities of their slaves to perform well, remained silent. The slaves, being well trained, knew better than to open their mouths.

"No questions?" Paul continued after a moment or two. "Then I will proceed with the demonstration. I would stress that I have not used this method of entertaining myself on Yasmin at any time in the past. It will be an entirely new experience for her."

So saying, he lit the three candles and moved to the side of the room to collect the tawse that lay on a table. He took up his position.

"Are you ready slave?"

The watchers saw Yasmin shudder with fear then brace herself. "I am ready, Master," she responded, her voice quivering.

Paul raised his arm and sent the tawse thudding across Yasmin's shoulders. She gasped at the impact and the watchers clearly saw her strive to force her body to remain static. The next stroke lashed across her full buttocks but, apart from another gasp, she showed no reaction. She managed to endure six strokes across each target area without moving.

As her back received its seventh stroke a cry of pain erupted from her throat quickly followed by another cry of despair as she flinched slightly forward and her breasts neared the flames, making her quickly jerk back. This movement caused the clamps to pull on her nipples and sex wringing yet another cry of despair from her. The next stroke across her buttocks produced the same reaction. So far, she had managed to take a total of fourteen strokes.

The next six strokes made her cries turn to screams and her body jerk more violently. Her breasts and sex had neared the candle flames each time the tawse lashed her body, wringing agonised screams from the slave and making her jerk against her chains, but, so far, she had not dislodged a clamp. Her back and buttocks were, by now, well marked with angry weals that shone dark red against her pale flesh.

Whether done deliberately or not, nobody ever discovered, but the next stroke of the tawse across her back came from an upward direction. The added pain caused by the tails crossing previous weals made Yasmin throw back her head and scream louder than ever. Her body jerked forward. Her already sore nipples pressed against the candle wicks, sending flashes of lightening through her breasts. The pain made her, instinctively, throw her body away from this source of agony. The wires to the clamps on her labia and nipples were pulled tight making her scream again and again as the teeth tore her tender teats and lips.

The watching slaves suppressed a groan of horror as they saw that both of the candles had gone out and both of the clamps on her labia had been torn free. Yasmin, her body streaming with sweat, collapsed as she hung in position, sobbing heavily as waves of pain washed through her body. Immediately Paul called for the test to cease, declaring that the demonstration had come to an end. He released the bonds on his slave's wrists and ankles and she sang in a sobbing heap on the floor, her hands frantically rubbing her tortured breasts and sex.

"As you can all see," Paul addressed the Masters, the test is a severe one and demands total concentration on the part of the slave."

He gave orders for the slaves to depart and wait in the lounge for their duties to recommence as usual and for the Masters to remain to discuss the demonstration.

With two of the slaves supporting her, Yasmin was taken from the Dungeon and up to the bathroom to clean herself and be made respectable while the remaining slaves made their way to the lounge in a stunned silence. They had all watched the demonstration with mounting dread, realising that if the Masters adopted Paul's suggestion, it would be them facing the ordeal in the future. Melanie, who had never yet been subjected to the candles and clamps was in a state of utter panic. She had seen how Yasmin had suffered and how she had made her suffering worse by her attempts to take as many strokes before ending the test. The very thought of those cruel sharp teeth biting into her most tender flesh, tearing at it as she writhed under the leathers, and the agony of the proximity of her breasts to the candle flames, was beyond her comprehension.

She tried to imagine herself, secured as Yasmin had been, while the cruel leathers lashed her back and buttocks. To do well in the test, she would have to remain static as the leathers inflicted agony on her body. The only way she could bring the ordeal to an end would be to voluntarily, thrust her tender flesh into the torment of the candle flames or to undergo the other agony of dislodging the clamps, causing equal agony to her sex and breasts. But, instinctively, she knew that if she went along that path, her Master would detect her stratagem and she wasn't sure she could cope with the disappointment he would feel.

The stunned silence was, eventually broken as the slaves all at once began to voice the thoughts that had coursed through Melanie's mind in the few minutes they had been in the lounge. At first, the slaves tried to convince themselves that Paul's suggestion would not be adopted but then, on remembering the looks on the watching Masters' faces, they realised that their hopes were in vain. They were slaves, whose sole purpose for existence was for the pleasure of their Masters, and their hopes, and wishes, were of no consequence. Each, in turn, would have to suffer the test and endure the pain as best they could to please their Master.

The Masters gathered in Paul's study after the

demonstration. They discussed the possibility of introducing the test as part of the agenda for the monthly Meetings. Whilst they were all in favour, there were one or two who had doubts, mainly because they feared that their slaves would be permanently damaged by the ordeal. Seeing that this was their only objection, Paul summoned Yasmin to their presence and allowed them to closely inspect her body. Her breasts and sex, whilst looking raw where the clamps had torn her flesh and the candles had burnt her, showed no sign of permanent damage. It was agreed that the test would be introduced at the next Meeting. It was further agreed that until a slave had taken her turn in the competition the Masters would not use this form of discipline on her. Thus no slave would be given the chance to practice before her turn came.

The slaves trembled as they were informed of the decision. Melanie wondered how she would make out when her turn came. She had to wait until three months later to find out. She trembled with fear when at last at one particular Meeting it was announced that her name had been drawn from the remaining list. She remained dressed in her costume as the other slaves made their submission and appeared naked, their buttocks showing the marks of the attention they had received, in the lounge.

After lunch, she was taken to the dungeon where the other slaves and Masters awaited. With trembling fingers, she discarded her costume and took her place at the whipping frame. She was secured in place. She moaned as the clamps were fitted to her nipples and sex, feeling the cruel teeth bite into her tender flesh. As the candles were lit, she felt the warmth from the flames close to her body. She braced herself for the flogging to commence. Her Master for the weekend was none other than Stephen, the film director to whom Craig had hired her and Jenny for the whipping scene in the film he was making. He had seen her under the lash and was well aware of her level of endurance. Therefore he had no scruples about laying on the strokes with full force.

This Melanie soon discovered. She found it very difficult to remain static as the tongues of the tawse lashed across her back and buttocks. The force of the blows was, in itself, enough to drive her body forward under normal circumstances but she resisted as best she could. Nevertheless, on several occasions, she did move and felt the heat searing her nipples and the pull on the clamps as she jerked back to avoid them. In the end, she had managed to absorb twelve lashes each across her back and buttocks before the twenty-fifth broke her concentration and, with an even louder scream of pain and despair, her body thrust forward. Her uncontrolled effort to avoid the burning pain, made her body jerk back and she felt one of the clamps tear away from her nipple.

The test was called to a halt and she was released and collapsed on the floor, her small hands clutching her breasts through which waves of pain were flowing. Craig watched with pride as her name was placed in second place on the chart. Only one slave, a strong girl named Stephanie, had endured longer and that by only one stroke.

Yasmin and another girl, helped Melanie to the bathroom where they attended to her and, once she had composed herself, helped her repair her appearance. As she entered the lounge some half hour later, she was greeted with applause and it was only then that she learned that she had earned second place on the chart. A position she was to hold for several months.

CHAPTER 9.

Craig's business was expanding and spreading to several countries abroad. The first excursion was to the Near East and, following various trips there, he had not only established valuable contacts but had, in the process made several friends. One of these was an Arab prince by the name of Abdullah bin Youssef. During one evening, when business had been concluded, the two men sat together in the prince's palace discussing the profound differences between their own ways of life and of their countries.

Craig, who had done considerable research on the second topic, was astounded to learn that slavery was still practised in the more remote parts of the prince's kingdom.

Knowing by then that the prince could, when trusted, keep secrets, Craig confessed that this also occurred in his country. A lengthy debate followed during which Craig had to admit that the slaves in his country were only those who agreed to submit voluntarily. He cited his two slaves, Melanie and Jenny as examples.

Prince Abdullah showed considerable interest in this and sought more details. Towards the end of the debate, he made a remark that was to lodge in both of their minds. "One day, you will have to bring those girls to my country and I will show them what true slavery is like."

It was several months later that Craig was reminded of the remark. At the end of a lengthy telephone discussion that the Prince rekindled the matter.

"You remember the last time you visited my humble home I said your slaves, particularly the one named Melanie, should learn what real slavery is all about?"

"Yes, I remember," Craig replied.

"Well, certain facts have come to my attention that might provide the opportunity to do just that. Can you come over next month and bring your girls with you? Don't say anything to them in the meantime. Just pretend it is to be a normal holiday."

Craig, who had intended to visit the Prince again in the near future, saw this as the perfect opportunity and details were agreed between them.

Two days before the departure date, Craig summoned the two girls to his study. He informed them that the three of them were to go away for a week or so. He gave them the instructions that had been decided between him and the Prince and sent them off to resume their duties.

The instructions gave both girls considerable food for thought. They were to wear no underclothes for the journey. This was not so unexpected. They were to take only one change of clothing, suitable for a hot climate and their slave costumes and their perfume, make up and toilet things. This, especially the inclusion of their costumes, made them wonder just what sort of holiday this was to be!

They set off at dawn on the morning of departure and Craig drove to the airport. Having entrusted the car to an attendant, he led them through Customs and the security check but, instead of heading for the normal departure lounge, they followed him along a corridor to a door which gave on to the concourse. A plush limousine was waiting for them and they wee driven to the private part of the airport and conducted on to a large private jet. As soon as they were settled in comfortable seats, the engines were started and the aircraft began to ease forward. Almost before they realised it, they were airborne and the plane had ascended above the thin layer of clouds. A pretty air stewardess, and a male steward, appeared and served them drinks and sweets.

The journey lasted several hours during which they were served with a delicious meal, more drinks and anything that they cared to ask for. Craig gave them no idea about where they were headed and the girls knew better than to seek enlightenment. Finally, they sensed the plane descending. They looked out of the windows and saw that they were approaching what appeared to be an airport close to a large town. All this was surrounded by desert. The girls were becoming a little apprehensive. From the appearance of the buildings, and taking into account the time they had been in the air, they realised they were landing at some remote arab city.

The plane taxied to a halt and the steward requested that they alight. As the door was opened the heat struck them like a blow. They descended the steps where another limousine awaited them. They were ushered into this and once their luggage had been put into the boot, it set off across the concourse. The vehicle was air conditioned and, after the brief encounter with the heat on leaving the plane, it was very comfortable. The journey took them from the airport, along a wide tarmac road with the desert stretching for miles on either side until they approached the large town they had seen as the plane descended.

On entering the town, they were intrigued by the town's architecture. The buildings were mainly one or two storeys in height and were of a dazzling white. Most of the ground floors were open in the front and they could see that these were shops, the stocks of which were on display on stands on the pavement, with the owners either sitting inside or busily working at their various crafts. All the people they saw were dressed in arab garments with the women hidden beneath long flowing robes with a hood that covered their faces except for a narrow gap through which they could see where they were going.

As the vehicle made its way through the bustle, they saw a large building standing on top of a slight hill. As they approached this they saw that it was surrounded by a high stone wall which was windowless and had only one large door. As they neared this the door, which was of solid wood swung open and they passed through. Immediately the scenery changed. A long drive led away from the door between bright green lawns with flower beds containing masses of flowers of many colours. The contrast between this and the surrounding country was startling. At the end of the drive, was the building they had seen from a distance. Close to, it was even larger than hey had imagined. Large windows, wide open, and doors, also open, gave on to the delightful lawns. The car stopped at the base of a short flight of steps at the top of which a door opened and an impressive figure emerged.

Craig, alighting from the car, was greeted by the man who he introduced as Prince Abdullah bin Youssef. He was to be their host for their stay. After introductions had been completed, the prince turned to the door and summoned the figure that was standing inside in shadow. Melanie and Jenny caught their breath at the apparition that approached down the steps. The prince was dressed in fabulously rich robes but, in contrast, the man who came towards them was dark skinned and naked except for a pair of bright red baggy trousers held up by a wide belt around his waist that sparkled with semi precious stones. But it was the curled whip, and the long cane, that hung from the belt that made them gasp.

The prince introduced the man as his major-domo, Sayed, and ordered the man to take the two girls to the harem and attend to them. Picking up their light luggage, the two girls apprehensively followed the man. He led them into the building and along corridors until they came to a heavy door beside which two more fierce looking men stood guard with scimitars held across their bare chests. Like Sayed, these men looked immensely strong with muscles on their arms, legs and chest standing out proud. Sayed knocked on the door and called out something in a language the girls did not understand. Slowly the door opened and Sayed ushered the two inside.

They entered a large room, beautifully decorated with the far wall made of large glass doors which stood open and through which they cloud see a wide lawn with a fountain in its centre and surrounded by beautiful flower beds, the scent of which drifted into the room on a gentle breeze to mingle with the other perfumes that permeated the air. The room was occupied by about thirty young females, all very beautiful and all looking at the new arrivals with unconcealed interest. Some of the girls were dressed in transparent baggy trousers, caught in at the ankles and through which their shapely limbs were visible, while others were stark naked. There were one or two men, dressed as Sayed but not so expensively, wandering about the room. Sayed summoned one of the girls who ran quickly to him and fell to her knees in front of him.

"This creature," he said turning to his guests, "Is Sacha. She speaks your language and will look after you during your stay. If she displeases you, let me know and she will be whipped." So saying, he turned and departed from the room.

Sacha remained kneeling until the major-domo had made his exit. Then she rose and looked closely and suspiciously at Melanie and Jenny.

"You have joined the Master's harem?" she asked in a low husky voice, full of suspicion.

"No," Melanie replied. "We come from England and are here for a short visit. Our own Master is a guest of the Prince."

Immediately the suspicious look departed from Sacha's face to be replaced by a friendly smile. Clearly she, like the other girls who had also looked suspiciously at the new arrivals, feared competition from them. With this threat removed, their attitude became more friendly. Sacha, having enquired their names, proceeded to conduct them from one girl to another, introducing them and stating the reason for their presence. She led them out onto the lawn and, out of the hearing of the loitering eunuchs, warned them not to touch the flowers, nor the fruit, growing on the bushes in one corner of the garden.

"These belong to the Master and, if we are seen even touching them it would earn us a severe whipping."

"Just for picking a peach?" Jenny asked.

"Yes," Sacha said. "Discipline in the harem is very strict and the eunuchs are on constant vigil. For minor offences, they can beat us with up to six strokes of the cane, which we must bend over for and take without moving. If we move, or for more serious offences, they report us to Sayed. He can then order us taken to the punishment yard where we are flogged with any implement of his choice. Certain offences are reported to the Master. Then the decision regarding the ensuing punishment is in his hands. Whilst he is very fair, it is not wise to be taken before him. The punishments he orders are severe and are to be avoided at all costs."

Melanie and Jenny digested this in silence. They wondered if, during their stay, they would be subject to the same discipline. After a short discussion between the two, they decided they probably would be, so vowed not to risk finding out.

They spent several days in the harem. The hours passed slowly, for there was nothing to do but laze round, eat at meal times and stay out of trouble. The ever present eunuchs curtailed any activity that might appear suspicious to them. Melanie and Jenny felt self conscious most of the time. They were still dressed in their European clothes and, due to the high temperature in the building, envied those who were scantily dressed, or naked. Several times during those days, one of the harem girls was summoned forward by one of the eunuchs, made to bare her buttocks if necessary and take a caning. Those girls managed to do so without moving although their cries of pain echoed round the room.

Once, a girl was summoned by Sayed and taken away. She returned an hour later, unable to walk and dragged by the arms by two eunuchs, and placed facing one of the marble columns that supported the ceiling. Her arms were pulled above her head and secured by the wrists to a ring. She was sobbing and naked, her exposed back and buttocks clearly showing signs that she had been soundly whipped. The poor girl was left there for several hours as a warning to the others. Sacha told the two visitors that the girl had been punished for disobeying one of the eunuchs. When the slave had served her time at the column, she was released and two of the other slaves, her closest friends, helped her to one of the side rooms where they attended to the weals on her body with soothing unguents.

Melanie and Jenny found life in the harem extremely boring. There was nothing to do but laze around, or to walk in the garden. The girls were not encouraged to spend too much time in the open, to prevent their soft skin being damaged by the rays of the sun. They tried to alleviate the boredom by singing and dancing. Several were accomplished with various stringed instruments. The ever present presence of the eunuchs prevented any disturbance but the two guests soon felt an undercurrent of jealousy and envy that quietly seethed beneath the apparent placid atmosphere. Each evening, the girls, having attended diligently to their appearance, were paraded before Sayed who chose the slave who would serve the Prince for the night. This honour was greatly sought after and was the main cause of the jealousy that was a part of harem life. If a girl was lucky enough to become pregnant, it meant her elevation from a slave to that of a concubine.

Since their arrival, the two girls discovered that, each

evening, two girls were selected. That one was to serve their own Master, Craig, was explained to them by Sacha. This caused both girls no end of misery – thinking that another was enjoying the pleasure that they thought was their own prerogative. They longed for the visit to end so they could return to their normal lives.

It was with a sense of relief that one morning they were taken from the harem and brought to a large richly furnished room where the Prince and Craig awaited them. They dropped to their knees before the seated men.

"Our stay here is to be interrupted," Craig told them. "My friend, the prince, has arranged for us to visit one of his sheiks in a distant part of his kingdom. Your baggage has been taken care of and we are now to be conducted to the helicopter that will transport us to our destination."

On his order, the girls rose and followed the men from the building to where the means of transport awaited. They climbed aboard and fastened themselves into the seats indicated. The aircraft took off and rose high into the air. Never having been in a helicopter before, both girls were nervous. The thing seemed so fragile and they expected to crash into the ground at any minute. As they looked out of the windows, they could see nothing but barren desert stretching for miles.

The trip took two hours, during which they passed over one or two small areas of vegetation. Apart from these, they saw nothing but the desert until the saw what turned out to be a large town in the distance. When they got near this, the helicopter descended and landed on a circular area of tarmac close to a small building. They were ordered to alight and get into a limousine that drew up beside the plane.

The limousine carried them to another large building, not so opulent as the prince's. Here the girls were again separated from Craig and conducted to the sheik's harem.

So began yet another period of boredom that taxed the girls' patience. However there was nothing for them to do but accept their lot and try and wait out the time until they returned to their own country.

Two mornings later, Melanie was sitting out in the garden, enjoying the sunshine and the beautiful flowers, when a eunuch, one that she had not seen before, approached her and ordered her to follow him. He led her from the harem and along several corridors until he came to a door. This he opened and pushed her inside, closing and locking the door behind her. She looked round. She was in a small dark room, devoid of any furniture. The silence worried her and she began to wonder why she had been brought there. The minutes dragged by and her wonderment grew into fear.

She was startled when a door in the wall opposite that by which she had entered the room, opened and two eunuchs entered. Without any preliminaries, they approached her in silence. Suddenly, she was grabbed by one and, as she was restrained, a rolled up piece of cloth was forced into her mouth and tied in place by a strip of material behind her neck. A thick black hood was thrust over her head. Despite her struggles, her wrists were manacled together behind her and her ankles tied together. She felt a cloak put over her and she was lifted over the shoulders of one of the eunuchs and carried from the room.

After some time, the eunuch took her from his shoulder and dropped her, unceremoniously, onto a hard wooden surface. As there was a sudden jolt and she felt forward motion, she realised that she was in some sort of cart. She began to panic and struggled to free herself but her efforts were in vain. Fortunately for her comfort, the journey did not last long and, when the cart halted, she was lifted out and again, thrown over the shoulders of some large man. After a short while, she heard a door open and she was stood on her feet. The cloak and hood were removed and she saw that she was in another small room with the two eunuchs. Fear swept over her. Had she been abducted? If so, by whom and why?

Her ankles were unfettered and the gag removed.

"Who are you? Why am I here?" Through her fear, anger made her braver than she really felt and the questions shot like bullets from a machine gun from her mouth.

Before she could issue another word, one of the eunuchs slapped her hard across her face, making her stagger back and fall to the floor.

"You will speak only when spoken to," the eunuch who had hit her shouted. "And then only in the most respectful and submissive terms."

Melanie, now in a state of absolute terror, looked up at the men, seeing that total lack of humanity in their faces. What she had, initially, thought of as a joke on Craig's part, no longer seemed to be such.

"Stand up and strip naked," the eunuch ordered.

"No!" Melanie shouted back.

The eunuch, the one who had not remained silent throughout, signalled to his fellow who grabbed hold of her and lifted her to her feet. The two dragged her from the room, along a corridor and into another room. They halted in the centre of the room and in front of them was a glass covered pit.

"Look down," the eunuch commanded.

Melanie did so and her heart leaped into her mouth and she felt the blood drain from her face in horror. Under the glass, several feet down, the floor was covered in a mass of writhing snakes.

"One more instance of disobedience from you and you will be put in with the snakes," the eunuch stated. "They are not fatally poisonous but their bite can cause extreme agony which, if not treated in time, can lead to madness."

The two eunuchs turned her round and frog marched her back to the first room. Melanie was terrified. This was no longer a joke on Craig's part. Did he know what had happened to her? Was he searching for her even then? But what worried her more was how did they know of her abject fear of snakes? Was it merely guesswork on their part or could they, somehow, read her mind.

"Strip!" the first eunuch repeated the order.

This time, Melanie did not hesitate but quickly obeyed, casting her few garments to one side and stood naked facing them. They walked slowly round her, inspecting her and using their hands to assess her body.

"It is a pity she is not a virgin," one said. "Her price would be considerably higher."

"Still, she should fetch a reasonable price once she is displayed on the auction block," the other replied. "Provided she does not misbehave."

"Have no fear of that," the first said. "Before she goes to the block, it will be made very clear to her what fate awaits her if she does not do as she is told."

The mention of price startled her. It seemed that they intended to sell her. Sell her in a slave market! She began to shake with terror. She was grasped by the arm and led from the room to yet another where a bath of hot water awaited her. She was ordered to lie along a wide table. A foaming lather was spread all over her body and one of the eunuchs, using a cut throat razor, proceeded to shave her body and limbs, removing all the hair from her skin except for that of her pubic bush. Melanie stayed rigid, only moving in accordance with their orders, fearful of the razor cutting her. Once this exercise was completed, she was ordered into the bath and to wash herself thoroughly.

She was given no time to enjoy the luxury of the bath. Once they considered she was clean, she was ordered out and given a towel with which to dry herself. They took her to another room where she was ordered to stand still in its centre. One of the eunuchs began to take measurements of all parts of her body, while his associate wrote the figures down on a clipboard. Her breasts were weighed and the size, and resistance, of her anus and sex were tested. Her teeth were examined and counted. The colour and length of her hair, both on her head and her pubes were entered on the board. Once the assessment was completed, she was ordered to lie down on a divan and one of her wrists was attached to a manacle on a short chain fixed into the wall. Ordering her to rest, the two eunuchs retired from the room.

She looked round her surroundings and saw that, apart from the bed, the only other items of furniture in the room were a dressing table, with a mirror attached, and a stool. On the dressing table were a brush and comb and several items of cosmetics. It seemed that she was to be made to attend to her appearance and beautify herself ready for the sale.

The sale! Surely they did not really intend selling her? She was not one of the girls from their country. She was a European and Europeans were not sold these days. Then she remembered that she had been told that if Craig had sold her to Stephen, he would have probably sold her abroad when she had served his purposes. So this was no dream. She was to be taken to the sale room, displayed for the scrutiny of men and eventually sold to one of them. She would, to all intents and purposes, disappear off the face of the Earth. She would be owned by some stranger who would treat her in whatever way pleased him, or her. This last thought horrified her. To be owned by a woman! The games she had played with Jenny, making love to her and beating her, and being beaten by her, would bear no resemblance to the fate that awaited her if some woman succeeded in buying her.

With terrifying effect, these thoughts slowly sank into her brain. And, with the thoughts, came the reality of her position. She was a slave! A real slave! No longer serving Craig as a slave by her own wishes! Now she would lose all control over her destiny. She curled up on the divan and shuddered with terror, praying that Craig would suddenly appear and rescue her. Surely, once he found out about her disappearance he, and the Prince and his men, would search for her and, once found, a terrible retribution would be the fate of her abductors.

She loved Craig. He was the master that her body needed. He dominated her in the way she desired and, especially with the beatings he administered, she wished for no other life. The beatings were, most of all what she desired and needed. Without these, any other form of submission would be totally inadequate. In her heart, she knew herself to be nothing but a slave. But it was only with Craig as her master that this Utopia could be hers. She prayed that he would soon come and rescue her. Even if it meant a beating for the anxiety he had been caused. A beating she would welcome!

She knew not how long she was left there before the eunuchs reappeared. One carried a tray of food and drink which he placed on the dressing table. She was ordered to sit on the stool and feed herself. She remained on the divan, ignoring the order. For a moment or so, a pregnant silence filled the room. A silence that Melanie found both disturbing and threatening. Then the bombshell fell, shattering both her dreams and her hopes.

"You will do as ordered," one of the eunuchs broke the silence. "Your so-called Master, who you know as Craig, has tired of you. He has decided to get rid of you by selling you off to whoever is stupid enough to buy you. You are destined to disappear from the face of the Earth, into some secure harem where you will be nothing but a slave. Our

Master who deals in slaves, has been commissioned to sell you. He intends to get a good price for you so expects you to behave perfectly when placed on the block. If your price does not reach the reserve figure, you will be blamed and suffer terrible consequences. The snakes will be a welcome alternative to the tortures he will order for you."

Melanie felt as if she had been hit in the stomach with a sledge hammer. Craig had tired of her! He no longer wanted her! It was with his blessing that she was to be sold off! Suddenly, with the loss of all hope, any resistance she had felt disappeared. She knew that she was totally at the mercy of these strangers. She was now, in truth, nothing but a slave. Her fate was to be slavery totally different to the slavery she had imposed upon herself when she had submitted, of her own free will, to Craig as her master. Now, her own will counted for nothing. She was a slave whether she agreed to it or not!

She rose to her feet and sat at the dressing table. With the eunuch's threats hanging over her, Melanie ate the food and drank the water that had been placed in front of her. When she was finished, the tray was taken away and a woman brought into the room. She immediately set about applying the cosmetics to Melanie's face and body. Melanie cringed as rouge was applied to her nipples and areolas and black kohl carefully applied to her sex lips. Her body was sprayed with an exotic perfume and her hair brushed until it fell in shining waves down her back, then wound up in a coil and pinned to the top of her head.

Once the eunuchs were satisfied, several veils of gossamer were put on her, each carefully placed and fixed so that they could be removed, one by one, slowly revealing the beauty of her body. This completed, the eunuchs agreed that she was as ready as they could make her.

Clearly the time of the sale had approached and, perhaps for the first time the true reality of her position came home to her. She was just a slave. Worth whatever some person was prepared to pay for her. That that person would have no affection, let alone love for her was a foregone conclusion. She had wanted Craig to use a whip on her to teach her the real meaning of her slavery. But, on reflection, even the lash of the whip on her back and buttocks had not made her into a true slave. It had taken her abduction and these two eunuchs to teach her that! For the first time in her life, she really knew herself to be a mere slave, of no worth, and to be disposed of in any way whoever owned her thought fit. To her surprise, as much as she had been in love with Craig and delighted in being his slave, the unknown future that stretched before her gave her a strange sense of pleasure that she would have until that moment, strongly denied. To her intense astonishment, she found that she was looking forward to being displayed on the slave block.

CHAPTER 10.

The eunuchs manacled her wrists together behind her back and placed a heavy black cloak over her head and body. The hood covered her eyes and completely concealed her. She felt a chain looped round her neck and pulled tight. By this she was led from the room. Guided by one of the eunuchs at her side, she was led along several short passages until the procession reached a door. The eunuch leading her knocked and the door was opened and she was led through. She heard the door closed behind her. The cloak was removed.

Looking round, Melanie saw that she was in a large rectangular room with wooden seats along each of the two long walls with a line of metal rings set in the wall above. She supposed this was where the slaves were made to sit, and be secured by chains to the rings as they awaited their turn to mount the block and be sold. In the wall opposite the one by which they had entered, she saw another door. From behind his came the subdued murmur of voices. She decided that this must be the room in which the merchandise was kept waiting until it was their turn to ascend the block. Though the door from which the sounds came must be the auction room. The absence of any other females for sale, decided her that this must be a very special auction, in which she was the sole item to be sold. She began to shake with a mixture of fear and trepidation. To whom was she to be sold? Would the customers like her enough to pay over the reserve price? If not, what were the terrible tortures that would be inflicted upon her tender body?

She realised that she had no alternative but to behave herself and do her best to ensure that the price she fetched was to the slaver's approval. Anything to avoid the terrible tortures the eunuch had promised would be her lot otherwise. She felt more terrified, helpless and submissive than she had ever done before. So this was what it was like to be a slave in the real word of slavery. A shudder ran through her body. She began to wonder who was to be her future master, or mistress. Would he, or she, be kind to her? She doubted it! How would she manage when her new owner wanted to use he body, or beat her? It would not be the man she loved who would make her submit! That her future was to be hard to bear was in no doubt.

In her mind, she thought back over her short life, from the time Craig had first spanked her bottom to the present day. She had felt terribly despondent when the eunuch had said Craig had tired of her and had commissioned the slave dealer to dispose of her. It was true, she thought, he had never actually said that he loved her. He desired her body, both for sex and to thrash whenever he wished. He had awakened the latent need to submit in her character and introduced her to the whip. The whip that, she had thought, would make her into a real slave. How mistaken she had been! It had taken her abduction and his renouncement of her to show her that! Now she was to be put on a slave auction block, displayed naked and bid for by men, and women, who would own her.

She realised, with shock and surprise, that she did not fear the future, rather looked forward to it. Had she really loved Craig, or was it just her submission and her slavery, such as it had been, that she had been in love with? It came as an even greater shock to admit to herself that, as much as she did love him, it was the state of slavery, to which he had led her, that she loved most of all. Then she considered her future. Pure and utter slavery, in the most deepest and demanding meaning of the word awaited her. Humiliation and the cruelty of the cane and whip were to be her lot. That the man, or woman, who would shortly own her, would take her down that road was in no doubt. She just hoped it would be a man.

Her deliberations were brought to an abrupt halt as the door leading to the sale room opened and a cruel looking man, dressed in full Arab regalia stood in the doorway and beckoned to the eunuchs to lead her forward. Her time had come and she felt her legs shaking with trepidation. She was hauled to her feet and made to walk through the doorway. The door closed behind her. She looked round her. She was standing on a semi-circular raised platform on one side of a large room. There was a narrow space in front of the platform beyond which there were rows of seats stretching back to the far wall. To her surprise she saw that there were only about a dozen men and a couple of women in the auditorium and they were very expensively dressed, with many precious stones sewn into their garments. The two women, also, were expensively adorned and their fingers were dripping with jewels.

She was made to stand at the edge of the platform, facing the prospective buyers. The auctioneer looked at the clipboard that one of the eunuchs handed to him then raised his eyes to the buyers, who fell silent. The auction was about to begin.

"Ladies and gentlemen!" The auctioneer's deep voice sounded loud in the silent room "This afternoon, a very special piece of merchandise is to be offered. Since the item is a European, she is not being offered in the normal way in an open auction. When sold, she must disappear into a secret harem, never to be heard of in the outside world again. This is why a private sale has been decided on, to which only a very select number of customers have been invited."

The auctioneer paused to let the serious nature of his words sink in before continuing. "By special commission, I have, this afternoon, a very delectable piece of merchandise for your consideration. To my regret, the slave is not a virgin but, on the other hand, I have been assured that she has been well educated in the ways to please both men and women. Her present Master has found it necessary, on many occasions, to discipline her. All parts of her body are therefore well used to the attentions of the rod, switch and leathers. The fascinating thing about this slave is that once she has been beaten her prowess in bed is greatly enhanced."

Melanie had remained stationary throughout this speech. But she could not help her face blushing as the last attribute was announced. Craig had certainly not left out any details of her to the auctioneer.

"Ladies and gentlemen," the auctioneer continued. "The item I have for you is a white European female aged twenty three years. As you will soon see for yourselves, she is a delightful piece of slave meat and will, I am sure, give whoever is lucky to acquire her, many years of exquisite pleasure. In bed she is reputed to orgasm with great enthusiasm and to produce copious amounts of fluid. Under discipline, she can take much punishment in silence but when she breaks she sings like a lark."

The men and women sniggered at these last revelations and Melanie could see their interest mounting. She felt like a prize cow in a market place. No consideration was being given to her modesty and she was being presented just as if she was just any other animal. Animal! That was what she was being reduced to! She heard the auctioneer continue, reading out the information from the clipboard. Her face reddened even more as she listened to the most intimate details of her body being read out. As the last detail was announced, Melanie sensed one of the eunuchs at her shoulder.

"Remember the snakes!" he whispered in her ear.

"Now, ladies and gentlemen, what am I bid for this prime piece of slave meat?" the auctioneer continued. "Who will give me a hundred dinars?"

Someone in the audience must have made the bid. Slowly, other bids were made until the price had reached five hundred dinars. The auctioneer did not seem disturbed at this slow approach, or the low figure.

"Perhaps it would be better if the goods were displayed a little more openly," he said at last and a ripple of excitement ran round the audience.

He made a sign to the eunuch standing at Melanie's side. He reached forward and removed one of the veils, exposing her eyes and forehead. More bids were called. When the figure reached a thousand dinars, the eunuch removed a second veil, exposing her shapely legs. The bids began to flow quicker as the beauty of her legs gave the audience an indication of what else was hidden beneath the other veils.

As the bid reached five thousand dinars, the eunuch removed the third veil. Now the smooth sweetness of her arms was on show. Still the bids came. Then the veil covering her head was taken away and the audience saw her face. The frightened look in her eyes enhanced her beauty and, as the eunuch released her hair and let it fall, the bids began to come faster. Both the auctioneer and the eunuch knew how to gradually display their merchandise to the best effect! The bidding had now reached fifteen thousand dinars!

Melanie had stood static as the auction had progressed. She had no idea what the reserve price was. She realised, remembering the threat of the snakes and the torture, that it was in her best interest to encourage the bidding to continue. She slowly turned her head so that she looked at each bidder in turn, smiling sweetly as she did so. To her consternation, she realised also that both of the women were looking at her with unconcealed interest in their eyes and were bidding just as furiously as the men.

The eunuch released another veil, exposing her from the

waist upwards. The full and firm breasts were now on full view and the sweet narrowing of her body from her shoulders to her waist. Obeying the whispered instructions from the eunuch, Melanie slowly turned a full circle, showing her naked back to the bidders. The bids now came even more fast and furious. She heard bids of twenty five thousand dinars, then thirty thousand dinars called. She felt the eunuch's hands at her hips and braced herself as her final veil was removed. She now stood naked, fully exposed to the eyes of the bidders. The fullness of her hips, the nicely rounded swell of her belly seemed to have the effect of an electric shock on the audience. As she, again obeying the eunuch, turned slowly, the firm fullness of her buttocks was shown.

The eunuch whispered a series of instructions in her ear and, obeying them, Melanie adopted various poses that further displayed her body to perfection. Some of the poses were terribly embarrassing, especially when she was ordered to turn her back to the audience, bend over and reach behind her and pull her buttocks apart. She nearly forgot herself, and the threats, when the eunuch made her face the audience, with her feet wide apart, bend her knees forward and thrust her sex towards them. The eunuch reached for a whip that hung from his waist and reversing the handle, thrust it into her sex. The gasp of despair, and desire, that this forced from her throat made the remaining bidders smile with appreciation.

It was then that Melanie realised that the sale, and the spectacle she presented, had aroused her. The handle slid into her with ease and increased her needs until she was unable to stop herself from thrusting her body back and forward on the intruder. She groaned with frustration as the eunuch removed the handle and held it up for inspection. It shone with her juices that had, in the short time it had been inside her, soaked the handle.

The bidding that had until then slowed down, rose in intensity once more, several of those that had dropped out, rejoining the battle to own her. When the bidding reached seventy thousand dinars, only one woman and one black man were in contention for her body. Melanie began to inwardly panic. She didn't like the look of the woman, who was gross and had an extremely depraved and cruel look in her eyes, but on the other hand she had heard somewhere that the life of a white slave, owned by a black man, was something to be feared. The bids reached seventy five thousand dinars and both the woman and the man for a while seemed to think carefully before making a bid. To Melanie's horror, the last bid, that for seventy thousand, had come from the woman. The last thing Melanie wanted was to fall into that woman's hands.

Desperation flowed through her. She had to make the man out bid the woman. She turned so that she was facing the last man in the running. She could see the hesitation and desire in his eyes. Slowly she sank to her knees spreading them wide and sat back on her heels, her hands palm downwards on the floor at her side.

"Buy me Master," she said as sweetly as she could. "Would you not like to own this slave? Have her lovely white body serve you deliciously between your sheets? See her squirm and hear her scream her surrender to you as she writhed under your whip? Surely, whatever price you pay for me would be well spent for the pleasures I could bring to you."

With these last words, she slid her feet back until she lay prone on the floor, her arms spread sideways and her face to the floor. A stunned silence filled the room. Even the auctioneer and the eunuch were speechless. No slave had ever had the temerity to speak when on the block. The eunuch raised the whip and brought the lash down with a resounding report across her unsuspecting buttocks. Apart from a gasp of shock and pain, Melanie showed no other reaction to the blow. Another strike lashed across her buttocks, bringing forth the same reaction. The eunuch raised the whip to deliver another lash when a shout made him hesitate.

"Stop!" the man had shouted. "I bid eighty thousand dinars."

The auctioneer looked at the woman but she, clearly reluctantly, shook her head.

"Sold to the gentleman who bid eighty thousand dinars."

Melanie was hauled to her feet by the eunuch and led back into the side room.

She had been sold! Relief that the woman had not procured her swept through her. But the man, although he had not been ugly, was no oil painting and she had detected a cruel streak in his eyes as he had looked at her. Instinctively she knew that her life as his slave would not be an easy one. After a time, the man entered the room and Melanie fell to her knees in front of him. He ordered her to rise. He manacled her wrists together behind her back, put a long hooded cloak over her and a collar, with a lead attached. The hood completely covered her face and she stumbled, unable to see where she was going, as she was led by the leash from the room. She walked for some time, guided by the lead, passing along several corridors and negotiating some stairs until she was eventually halted. The collar and the cloak were removed and the collar then replaced round her neck. She and her leader, stood before a heavy door.

"Prepare to meet your new Master," her guide said.

"But, my Lord, I thought you were my new Master!" Melanie said, suddenly shaken by his words.

"I do not have that misfortune," her guide replied. "I was merely your new Master's agent, with orders to buy you at all costs. He has paid a high price for you, slut, so make sure he gets value for his money, or your life will not be worth a single dinar."

Her guide then knocked on the door and, when it opened, dragged her through. She was led into a large room. At the far end, a figure sat on a throne-like seat. It was clothed in the customary garb of an Arab noble, with its face hidden behind the headdress which had been drawn across its face in such a manner that not even his eyes could be clearly seen in the narrow slit that had been left uncovered. Melanie felt her legs begin to shake as she approached. He appeared so rigid and stern and she sensed that here was a man who would brook nothing less that complete and utter submission from her.

"Kneel before your Master," her guide ordered.

Slowly, seductively, Melanie sank to her knees, spreading them wide apart and her hands, palm down, on the floor at her side. She kept her eyes submissively lowered. She was about to discover what tribulations fate had in store for her.

"Tell your Master who you are."

"I am called Melanie," she said quietly. "I am my Master's slave."

"What duty do you owe to your Master?" the guide asked.

"Total submission, Sir. It is my duty to serve and please my Master, perfectly, in all ways, in all things and at all times," she replied.

"You were once owned by a man named Craig," the guide continued. "Was he your true Master? Did you love and serve him well?"

"I was a so-called slave to man called Craig, but I have come to learn, today, that he was not a true Master," Melanie responded softly. "But I hope I served him well, although he had to beat and whip me on many occasions. Yes, I did love him since he introduced me to my true self and started me on my journey to utter slavery."

"What was your true self?"

"To be nothing but a worthless slave, serving my Master's pleasure in any way he required," Melanie answered.

"He used a whip on you? Was it that which taught you the true meaning of slavery?" the guide said.

"I thought so," Melanie replied. "But I was wrong. The events of this day, being displayed naked, and auctioned before a group of strangers and sold as a slave taught me what real slavery was like. Now I know myself to be nothing but a complete and utter slave, subject to my Master's slightest whim." Melanie spoke voicing, perhaps for the first time, her true and deepest feelings. A slave must hide nothing from her Master and she now knelt before the man who would be just that.

"Raise your eyes and look upon the face of your true Master," the guide ordered.

Feeling her body trembling with fear, apprehension and expectation, Melanie obeyed.

The seated figure raised his hand and, slowly removed the part of the headdress covering his face.

Melanie gasped in shock as she looked into the face of her new Master. It was a face she knew well, except for the expression that stared back at her. It was Craig's face! She felt her senses whirl and feared she was about to collapse in a faint.

"But I was told you did not want me any more!" she blurted out. "How come I now kneel before you?"

Craig clapped his hands and a half naked eunuch entered the room. Craig turned to him. "The slave spoke without permission. Whip her!"

Before she realised what was happening, the new arrival grasped her by her arm, hauled her to her feet and pulled her to one of the marble columns that supported the ceiling. The manacle was released from her right wrist, her arms pulled round the column and the manacle reattached.

Glancing over her shoulder, Melanie watched in terror as the eunuch stepped back behind her and unclipped the coiled whip that hung from his belt. With a cry of distress, she turned her face away, pressing her cheek against the column.

Her body was flung against the marble as the lash whipped across her bare back. Her buttocks received the second stroke and she cried out in pain. Eight more times the lash curled, alternatively, across her back and her buttocks wringing screams of pain from the slave. After the tenth stroke, her wrists were released from the column and again secured in front of her. She sank to the floor and was dragged back in front of Craig. She collapsed, sobbing and heaving on the floor, not daring to look up at the men.

"Perhaps that sample lesson will teach the slave her station for the future," Craig said. "Remove her and take her to my quarters."

Melanie was hauled to her feet and led from the room. Her mind was utterly unable to comprehend what was happening to her. She had been discarded and sold yet, now, she found that she was still the slave of the man she loved. Her back and buttocks were on fire from the whipping he had ordered, yet she inwardly cursed herself for not having taken the beating better. She was left in a crumpled sobbing heap in the middle of a room that was obviously Craig's quarters. She knew not how long she lay there, slowly getting her sobbing under control, before the door opened and someone entered and sat down on a chair facing where she lay.

"Kneel up and look at me."

The command in Craig's voice broke the silence in the room. Hastily, ignoring the waves of pain that the movement caused in her back and buttocks, Melanie obeyed.

"Buy me Master," Criag said, imitating her voice. "Would

you not like to own this slave? Have her lovely white body serve you deliciously between your sheets? See her squirm and hear her scream her surrender to you as she writhed under your whip? Surely, whatever price you pay for me would be well spent for the pleasures I could bring to you."

Melanie felt her heat sink as he repeated the words she had uttered on the block. Either he had been there, witnessing her auction, or his minion had given him a word for word report on her conduct. She had begged, perfectly as a slave should do, for the stranger to buy her body for his pleasure. She felt her face turn hot and red with her shame.

"Now I will answer your question," Craig said, after a few minutes' silence. "By your own admission, the whip, as I had always suspected, did not reduce you to an utter slave as you said you desired. So I decided, with the Prince's assistance, to arrange for this afternoon's performance. You have now experienced what it is like to be rejected by the man you claim you love; to be auctioned off to a crowd of complete strangers to do with you as they wish; to debase yourself in public by acknowledging your slavery and begging to be bought. You will never, in the years to come, forget this day, will you?"

"No Master," Melanie replied.

Craig smiled inwardly at the sweet and submissive tone in her voice. Perhaps his plan had succeeded after all. Time would tell.

"As you well know, I do not love you. But I find your body and appearance pleasing and will, for the time being, keep you. But from now on, you will be nothing but the slave you have, this afternoon, declared yourself to be. You may rise and don your slave's costume."

Melanie saw that he pointed to a stool to one side of the room where her slave's costume and jewellery lay. As seductively s she could, she rose and put them on. Once her dressing was complete, she had to confess to herself that she felt entirely different to how she had done when wearing them before. Now she was, truly, a slave.

She was to continue to wear these adornments on her return journey to the Prince's palace and until it was time to prepare for the trip back to England. When this time arrived, it was with considerable reluctance that she changed out of them and into the clothes she had worn for the outward journey.

CHAPTER 11.

Craig's business was thriving and, although he had delegated a great deal of the routine, day to day, work to his office staff, he kept a close hands-on- approach. When possible, he worked from home, involving Melanie since he had, during her time in the office, developed a great deal of respect for her judgement and business acumen. He sometimes had to travel abroad and usually took Melanie with him. By doing so, he could make use of her brain and, when alone in their hotel bedroom, of her body. He always carried a cane, switch, cuffs and a ball gag in his luggage. After a heavy day's work, it was a relaxing pleasure to beat her and then slake his sexual desires. By turning the T.V. volume up and using the ball gag to mask her cries, he could beat her without disturbing the tranquillity of the other guests.

Ever since their return from the trip to the Prince's palace, she had behaved as a perfect slave girl. Even Ayesha noticed the difference in her and wondered what had occurred during the holiday to bring about this change. To Melanie's relief, she was never informed. It would have been just too humiliating for her to know that she had been placed on a slave auction block and slowly striped naked as men - and women, had bid to own her body and how she had behaved while this was being done to her.

The deepest natural instinct of a slave had been awakened in her by this experience and she conducted herself accordingly. But her spirit had not, to Craig's relief, been broken by the ordeal and she still committed many offences which earned her many a beating. To her delight, she was also beaten on many occasions for her Master's pleasure and she revelled in the marks these thrashings left on her body, especially when a whip was used.

It so happens, as things do, that two urgent problems

arrived on Craig's lap at the same time, both of which required travelling. The more important one was in England and the other in Paris. Neither could be put off so he could not attend to both of them himself. There was nothing for it but to send Melanie to Paris. He arranged with his office secretary to make the necessary travel and hotel arrangements and took the tickets and itinerary details home with him. The next morning, having pleasured himself with Jenny in the Correction Room and his bed the previous night, he summoned Melanie to his study.

"I have an urgent task for you," he told her. "It will mean you travelling alone to Paris and staying there for two nights. I will take you to the railway station in two hours. But first, there is something that must be done to keep your status firmly fixed in your mind. Follow me."

Melanie was initially perturbed at the idea of going on her own. It would be the first time she had done so since becoming his slave. With this concern on her mind, she followed him from the study. Her unease was deepened as he led her to the basement door and into the Correction Room. Once inside and the door closed, he faced her.

"This will be the first time you have travelled on your own and been away from me," he began. "So I am going to give you something to make sure you behave yourself and do not forget who you are, what you are, and who owns you while you are away. Strip."

Melanie was in no doubt as to what the 'something' could be and, with that usual tingling in her sex beginning, did as he had ordered.

When she knelt, naked, in front of him he continued. "You have done nothing wrong, that I am aware of, but a sound lashing with a whip across your backside will, I am sure, keep your mind focused on that fact that you are my slave. Stand under the chains."

Melanie rose and obeyed, halting where the chains were

suspended from the ceiling. She offered no resistance as he lifted each of her arms and clipped her wrist cuffs to the ends of the chains, stretching her arms straight above her head. He spread her legs apart and attached her ankle cuffs to rings set in the floor. She looked at her reflection in the wall mirror and thought that she made a very erotic picture, with her arms and legs spread wide, making it more difficult to turn as she was lashed. Her firm breasts were pulled upwards and, with her nicely rounded stomach with the auburn triangle of her neatly trimmed pubes she thought that she would do credit to any Pasha's harem.

She saw the look of fear appear in her eyes as she saw his reflection in the mirror, feeling the arousal mounting within her, as he took the single lash whip from its hook and took up his position behind her. This was something new to her for it was the first time he had beaten her neither for punishment nor pleasure, it was simply as a form of instruction. She saw him shake the lash loose and raise his arm. She braced herself as the lash sped towards her, only losing sight of it at the last minute as it was masked by her body. Then there was a sharp report and a line of fire blazed across her buttocks, making her gasp with the sudden pain.

Craig smiled with satisfaction as he saw the weal appear on her soft flesh that was, until then, unmarked, and a ripple flow outwards from the point of impact. Slowly, deliberately, he laid on four more lashes before, again closely inspecting his slave's buttocks. Five distinct livid weals now decorated her behind, each already rising into a burning ridge. He was not going easy on her as he intended that her behind would feel the pain for the days she was away! He was pleased to see the five weals were almost parallel, one below the other, displaying his expertise with a whip, even though Melanie had been unable to remain completely stationary, she had kept her back to him and the weals stretched round both sides of her cheeks.

She writhed and screamed her way through ten more lashes across her tender buttocks, concentrating on the lower part of the cheeks and the most tender areas just above where they joined with her thighs. That way, when she sat down, the pain would be more pronounced. After the fifteenth stroke had wrung a loud scream from his slave, Craig returned the whip to its place on the wall. He regarded his slave's bottom and smiled to himself in satisfaction. The marks, he would not allow Ayesha to treat them this time, and the pain would last for the days she would be away and be a constant reminder that she belonged to him. He allowed her a few minutes to compose herself before releasing her and ordering her to go and clean herself up and report to him in the study. He specifically informed her that she was not to have Ayesha perform her usual duty and apply cream to her behind.

Melanie, having duly thanked him for the whipping, as was always required, made her way gingerly to the bathroom. She dared a quick look at her bottom in the mirror and gasped as she saw the heavy raised weals that stood out from her flesh. She saw that he had, indeed marked her well. She would certainly carry the marks for the days she was to be away and they would be sore for at least a few days and, where he had laid those last five strokes, across the base of her cheeks, would be painful every time she sat down. She repaired her appearance and hurried down to his study.

Craig explained to her the details of the task she was to perform and the hotel and travel arrangements. To her surprise, he informed her that she was to be conventionally dressed, even to wearing underclothes. Although most of the expenses of the trip had already been taken care of, he provided her with sufficient money to cover incidental costs. He then ordered her upstairs where he supervised her packing. Finally, producing a suitcase, which contained the clothes she had been made to discard on her first arrival at his house, he made her dress. The feel of the underclothes on her body was strange and, surprisingly, uncomfortable. Not only because the knickers pressed tight against the weals on her backside.

He drove her to the station but, before sending her to catch the train, dropped the bombshell he had been saving.

"Remember that you are a slave and, although you will be firm in your negotiations, you will treat Pierre Dupont with respect. He is a bit of a lady's man and will no doubt find you irresistible. If the negotiations are concluded satisfactorily, and he makes advances to you, you will satisfy him. You understand?"

"Yes Master," Melanie replied. She was his slave and had no inclination to question his order. "But, if I do, he will probably see the whip marks on my bottom!"

"Then you will tell him that you were whipped for my pleasure," Craig replied to her astonishment. "If he pursues the matter further, then you may disclose our true relationship. He will not find it unusual, since he owns a slave of his own."

With this ringing in her ears, Melanie collected her small suitcase from the car boot and made her way on to the platform. Normally, the journey would have been reasonably comfortable. But her buttocks still burned from the whipping and every time the train crossed the points, the vibration sent sparks of renewed pain through her cheeks. Consequently, when the train eventually arrived at the terminus in Paris, she alighted with a sense of relief. She had been to Paris several times with Craig and knew her way around. The hotel was well known to her and she soon settled in. Once she had unpacked her case, she phoned Pierre Dupont, advised him of her arrival and confirmed their appointment for ten o'clock the next morning in his office. She partook of dinner in the hotel dining room and, in accordance with Craig's orders, spent a boring evening, alone, in her room.

The next morning she presented herself at Pierre's office on time and was conducted to his office. The negotiations were, as expected, protracted and he insisted in breaking off and taking her to lunch. Pierre was most attentive over the meal and Melanie became uneasy as it was made plain to her that he found her attractive. The afternoon saw her task completed. To her relief, she had conducted the negotiations with care and had obtained exactly what Craig required. Once the documents confirming this were signed, Pierre asked for the pleasure of Melanie's company for the evening. She accepted, since she had been warned this would probably happen.

Dinner at a top class restaurant drew to a close and, as Melanie expected, Pierre suggested they adjourn to his house for a nightcap. The house, unsurprisingly large since he was a wealthy man, was in the suburbs of the city. On arriving, she was shown into a large, expensively furnished lounge. Pierre pulled a bell cord and almost immediately, the door opened and an extremely attractive blonde entered. Melanie mentally put her age at abut thirty. She was dressed in a white, almost translucent Grecian style, gown that clung tight to her shapely figure, so tight that it was plain that she wore nothing under it, and displayed her pale seductive shoulders.

"You rang, Sir?" she spoke in a soft, respectful voice, although she had cast a quick questioning glance in Melanie's direction.

Melanie instantly recognised the submissive air about the girl and wondered if she was the slave Craig had said Pierre owned.

"My guest and I require drinks," Pierre replied, not saying 'please', which seemed to confirm Melanie's assumption of the girl's standing.

In a very respectful manner the girl enquired of Melanie what she would like and, when Melanie replied, served them. The task completed, she knelt at the side of Pierre's chair. Pierre was a good conversationalist and the evening progressed in a pleasant manner. But Melanie felt uneasy after having been a slave for so long, as Pierre treated her as an equal. Only the girl kneeling at his side, gave any indication that he was used to women being slaves. At the back of Melanie's mind, however, lurked the thought that he might make advances to her. When she thought it was time to return to her hotel, she asked if he would call a taxi for her.

"There is no need for that," he said, a gleam appearing in his eyes. "You can stay here for the night and I will run you back to your hotel in the morning. Yvonne can lend you anything you may require."

Melanie was about to say that it would not be necessary for her to stay as the hotel was expecting her back. The words were forming on her tongue when she saw the stern expression appear on Pierre's face, almost as if he could read her mind. Instead she gave in and thanked him for his hospitality. It was not long afterwards that Pierre announced that it was time to retire. Yvonne showed her upstairs to the guest room and provided her with the necessary toiletries and, wishing her; 'Good night,' went from the room, leaving her alone.

It was only after the door had closed that Melanie realised she had no pyjamas or nightdress. She thought of calling the girl back then changed her mind. She was, after all, used to sleeping naked. She washed, cleaned her teeth and undressed. She was on the verge of getting into bed when, without warning, the door opened and Pierre and Yvonne walked in. Pierre was dressed in an expensive silk dressing gown and Melanie suspected he wore nothing beneath it. Yvonne was, on the other hand, stark naked and Melanie gaped on surprise as she could see that the girl's pubic hair had been shaved off.

On their entry, Melanie's arms and hands had flown to her body, one hand covering her sex and the other across her breasts. Then, remembering what she was, she let them fall to her sides.

"Such modesty!" Pierre said laughingly. "And in a slave too! We thought you might like some company."

So Craig had already told Pierre of her status! Melanie, once he had arranged for her to stay the night, had expected something like this but not that he was already aware that she was a slave. What she had not expected either was that the girl would come with him. Pierre sat down on a chair and, with a smile on his face, watched as Yvonne approached their guest and put her arms round her, at the same time planting a lingering kiss on her lips. Melanie, being used to being kissed by Jenny, did not resist, even when she felt Yvonne's hands slide down her back and cup the cheeks of her buttocks.

"So, you were whipped also," Yvonne whispered in her ear as she pressed the hard weals on Melanie's buttocks. "That is good! Now we will both be ready for the Master. I find a good whipping prepares my body perfectly, don't you?"

Before Melanie could respond she was pressed backwards to the bed. The end of the bed against the back of her knees made her lose her balance and she fell, on her back, onto the soft duvet. The kissing mouth fell away and soft fingers stroked her sex. Her body had been well trained by her Master and immediately she sensed the beginnings of an arousal in her belly.

Instinctively, she put her arms round the girl and her hands touched the girl's back. She gasped as she found that the expected soft smooth flesh was decorated with long hard ridges which stretched the full width of the girl's back. She had been recently whipped, very recently judging by the heat that still emanated from the weals. But she had no further time to dwell on the discovery as Pierre, having discarded the robe, joined the couple on the bed.

What followed during the next hour or so was to stay in Melanie's memory for some time to come. Pierre made full use of all three of her orifices. While he was thus engaged, Yvonne's fingers probed deep into the recesses that Pierre was not using at the time. Melanie gasped in surprise when she felt Yvonne's tongue inserted between her swollen labia and then between her buttocks and into her anus as Pierre's rampant penis thrust against the back of her throat. Jenny had never, as yet, tried that one on her! A bolt of exquisite lightning shot through her as the girl's sharp teeth closed on her clitoris and bit it gently.

In her turn, completely engulfed in the tide of sexual passion, Melanie used her fingers and tongue on every part of the other two bodies, tasting the flavour of the places where their tongues and fingers had been, both inside her and each other. She lost count of how many times she and Yvonne screamed in pleasure as shattering orgasms flowed through them. Much later, Melanie marvelled at the supreme control Pierre managed to exert on himself as it was only when both girls' stamina was fully spent that she felt him, with a shout of elation, jettison his sperm deep into her womb, sending her into one final, exhausting orgasm. All too soon, it seemed to her, Pierre and Yvonne arose from the bed and, wishing her, 'Pleasant dreams' made their way from the room. Melanie sank into a satiated, but exhausted, sleep. .

She was awakened by a maid the next morning and, after a shower, she dressed, made herself up and descended to the dining room where, to her surprise, a full English breakfast was ready. She had never felt so hungry and set to with gusto, as did Yvonne and Pierre. Melanie was somewhat surprised that Pierre ate at the same table as the slaves but, as he explained, this was a special occasion. After breakfast, Melanie and Yvonne hugged and kissed each other as goodbyes were said. Pierre drove her back into town and halted outside her hotel.

"I will confirm our business agreement to Craig by letter today," he said. "I will also congratulate him on possessing so attractive and satisfactory a slave. Your behind looked very nice with the marks still fresh. " Melanie felt herself blush at this reference to the previous night's activities. "I will also ask him to let me have first refusal if he ever decides to sell you. Au revoir!" So saying he let in the clutch and sped off into the busy traffic.

Melanie stood dumbfounded on the pavement. That was the second time, to her knowledge, that someone had referred to Craig selling her. That was something she must take up with him as soon as she could. Surely he would not try and sell her? Would she submit if he did? Would she be given a choice? With these worries churning in her mind, she turned and entered the hotel. She was half way across the reception area when she heard a voice call out. "Melaina". She halted in her tracks, not believing her ears. It had been years since she had heard that name spoken! She turned her head and saw two men moving quickly towards her.

She panicked! She made a dive for the lift, just as the doors were closing. Fortunately, the lift was nearly full and stopped at almost every floor before reaching hers. She quickly entered her room and closed, and locked, the door. She sat on the bed and tried to pull herself together. She was in dreadful danger.

She had been born Princess Melaina Stroskova, a distant relative to the ruling family of a small Eastern European country, a fact which she kept as a closely guarded secret. She had changed her name to Melanie Browne when she had escaped from the tyrannical rule of an aged uncle who was intent on marrying off her to an equally tyrannical friend who desired her solely for her lovely body. Her uncle, she had no doubt, fully intended to capitalise on the man's infatuation and had given his blessing to the proposed union. He had made no secret of the fact that he would also greatly benefit financially. Melanie's protests and pleas against the marriage fell on deaf ears. The only course open to her had been to disappear.

'Get a grip on yourself!' she told herself. Think! Somehow she must evade the men below. Even the fleeting glimpse she had of them had been sufficient for her to recognise at least one of them as a thug employed by her uncle. If they found her again, they would kidnap her and take her back to their employer. A fate she could not contemplate. The panic had gone and she was thinking straight. An idea came to her. She phoned down to the reception desk and said she had a serious complaint and asked for the manager to come to her room immediately.

The hotel enjoyed a good reputation and this brought the manager to her room within a few minutes. Quickly she apologised for the subterfuge and told him that there were two men in the reception area that had been molesting her. She did not want the police brought into the matter and asked if the manager could arrange for a taxi to wait for her at the hotel's tradesmen's entrance at the rear. The manager, also happy not to involve the police agreed and phoned down to make the necessary arrangements.

Five minutes later, the phone rang to inform her that the taxi was there. The manager, carrying her case, led her down and out the back way and the taxi speedily carried her to the train terminal. She had a few anxious minutes, looking back along the platform for signs of pursuit before the train drew away from the platform. She collapsed into her seat, breathing a sigh of relief. But the near encounter had unnerved her. She had thought herself safe in her new life but the happiness she had found seemed now to be threatened.

Arriving back home, she was surprised to find Craig there and not in his office. Pierre had obviously telephoned that morning and he was pleased with the result of her trip. He led her into his study and demanded that she told him everything that had taken place. Melanie obeyed. When it came to relating the events of the previous evening, she was nervous that he would not approve of her conduct. But, as it turned out, he was both interested and not displeased, even saying that he would try the three in a bed sessions himself.

When she came to the part of her story concerning the two men in the reception area of the hotel, he became serious and pensive. The thought that she might have been abducted and taken away from him caused him no end of concern. Whilst he did not actually love her, he certainly did not want to lose her. She was too perfect a slave for that to be allowed to happen. No doubt he could, if he wished, find another to take her place but he did not want that sort of aggravation to disturb his life. Anyway, it would be doubtful if another would satisfy his requirements as well as she did. He said to leave the matter with him and he would give it some serious thought.

Melanie went and changed into her slave's costume and continued with her duties. It was lovely to be dressed again as she should be. The trip had been enjoyable, but being dressed in conventional attire had seemed strange and unnatural to her. Also she was grateful that someone else would have her immediate problem in hand.

It was late that day that he recalled her to his study.

"I have decided on a course of action that will prevent any of your uncle's henchmen from interfering with you ever again," he began, and Melanie breathed a silent sigh of relief. "You are fully aware that, whilst I find you extremely satisfying as a slave, I do not love you. That you, as you say, love me is exactly how a slave should feel about her Master. You and I will get married. That will both bind you to me securely and, at the same time, negate any use your uncle might have for you. Marrying me is not a command. You are at liberty to refuse, without fear of retribution. Go away. Think about it and I will ask for your answer tomorrow evening."

Melanie managed to keep her mind on her work all the next day. It had not been necessary to think about her answer. But if she were to marry him would it alter their relationship. She could not marry him if it meant that she would no longer enjoy a life as his slave. She thought about this for a while and a daring scheme came to her mind. A scheme which, she knew, would result in her suffering agonies, the cause of one being, at that time, beyond her imagination. But she had to endure it to ensure that her future as his wife would be in accordance with her heart's desires. Finally, after spending some minutes in her room writing down her demands if she agreed, she felt she had solved all her problems. She hid the paper away safely to await his summons that evening. It came just after the evening meal had been cleared away and she had helped Ayesha and Jenny with the dishes. Again, she stood before his desk, the paper clutched on her hand.

"Well? Have you made your decision?" he asked.

"Yes, Master," she replied. "I would be honoured and grateful to become your wife. But there are conditions, dare I say demands, to which you must agree and to which you will adhere for ever. First is that I also remain your slave and that you always treat me as such. Second is that you are stricter with me than you have been so far and, since it will be my duty, both as a slave and a wife, to please you in all ways, at all times, that you make my punishments more severe. Third is that, as well as the normal wedding ceremony, once we return from honeymoon, if we have one, there will be a second ceremony in accordance with the details I have written on this paper." So saying, she handed him the paper on which she had written her demands.

Craig studied the paper for some time. Melanie, her heart in her mouth with anxiety, watched his face carefully, but it remained expressionless. Finally, he put the paper down and raised his eyes to hers. Her heart missed a beat as she saw the lust in his eyes.

"I agree to all of your demands except one," he said, to her immense relief and joy. "The one exception is the final part of this ceremony. I do not think it right for your body to be permanently marked, especially in this fashion which would be extremely painful."

"But Master," Melanie interrupted. "I am - as you well know a mere slave, your slave, and since you have decided to keep me for ever, it is only fitting that my body bear the sign of your ownership. It is part of the ceremony and you must accept it in its entirety or not at all."

"All right!" Craig conceded. "But your body must be numbed first."

"No Master," Melanie replied, sternly. "I know it will be painful but if it is to have any meaning, I must feel it done. I insist."

"But father might think otherwise," Craig said.

"Then you must persuade him to agree," Melanie insisted.

"All right! If that is what you want. But it is not for a slave to make demands on her Master. A matter that I will deal with at a later date! Right now there is a more pressing concern to be dealt with. Report to the Correction Room in ten minutes."

"Yes, Master," Melanie replied and made her way from the room. As she prepared herself, she felt waves of happiness flow over her. Her Master had agreed to her demands and, once the ceremony was completed, she would be his slave for the rest of her life. Also the summons to the Correction Room could only mean a flogging and it was something she had wanted more than anything while she had been away.

Ten minutes later, with her stomach all of a flutter, Melanie knocked on the Correction Room door. As she entered, she was surprised to note that both Jenny and Ayesha were not there to witness her punishment. She knelt before her Master.

"It seems that you have been deceiving me for some time," Craig began. "You have kept your true identity and origins from me. You are aware that a slave is not permitted to have secrets from her Master. A lesson I am about to impress on you now. Since I do not wish the other two to know of what is now our secret, they will not be present. If asked, you will say that you were beaten for my pleasure to celebrate your return. Understood?"

"Yes, Master," Melanie replied, grateful for his guarding her secret. The fewer people that knew it the less the chance of it being discovered!

They went through the normal punishment routine and Melanie soon stood under the suspended chains, her wrists secured to them above her head and her small hands gripping the chain tightly. She writhed and screamed in pain and happiness as the single thong whip lashed across her back and buttocks until her throat was hoarse and the only sound she could make was a gasp and moan each time a stroke was applied.

She lost count but she had taken fifteen lashes across each area before Craig stood in front of her and laid another ten strokes across her breasts and stomach.

When Craig eventually released her wrists from the chains, she sank into a quivering heap on the floor. She was happy. She was again under the control of her Master and, so sure was she of his ownership of her, the threat she had encountered in Paris dwindled into the background. That Craig would lose no time in arranging for their marriage, she had no doubt and then after the second ceremony she had planned, she would for ever after be his slave and her destiny would have been fulfilled.

Up stairs in the bathroom, once she had been dismissed from the Correction Room, she regarded the reflection of her body in the mirror. Her back, bottom, breasts and stomach all bore the evidence of the severe whipping she had just received. She looked at the weals with pride. Before she turned away, she wondered whereabouts on her soft body her Master would put the mark of his ownership. It had been necessary to involve his father and Julia in her scheme and she prayed that, if she begged them hard enough, they would not only consent to take part but also to do so without any thought to her suffering. Suffering that she would welcome with as much happiness as when her Master used her body to slake his sexual desires.

She was not beaten again before their wedding and, by then, her body had lost all signs of the whipping. Since she had no father to give her away, Alex happily performed this duty. Julia and Jenny acted as her Maids of Honour. As she stood by Craig's side and made her vows, she could not help thinking of the other vows she would make on their return from honeymoon when the second ceremony would take place. Vows which she would make with as much, if not more, pleasure as those she was making then. She smiled inwardly as she felt her soft buttocks tremble at the thought of what they would then have to endure.

ADULT FICTION
Silver Moon

The **Vicar's Daughter**

Richard Garwood

The Vicar's Daughter.
A girl wakes in a strange bedroom with no recollection of how she got there. And the strangeness increases as she comes to realise that the girl she sees in the mirror, is a very different one to the girl she remembers being!

What ensues is a deeply erotic journey of self-discovery that leads her down the paths of submission......

Dear John.
A sea cruise like no other is revealed bit by bit in a series of letters home! Richard Garwood's original and vivid imagination creates erotic scenes and performances that transform the heroine in page after page of intensely erotic action.

Two erotica-packed novellas in one volume!

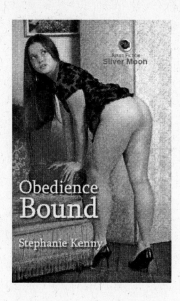

Obedience
Bound

Stephanie Kenny

When Claire comes to in hospital after a minor traffic accident, she finds that her behaviour seems to have altered dramatically. She also finds that she is the focus of attention of a mysterious stranger who commands her sexually in a way she has never experienced before.

As she recovers he leads her into more and more extreme encounters that she finds herself taking more and more pleasure in. But then she goes on holiday with her husband and he disappears just as the mysterious 'X' makes ever more stern calls on her body.

Stephanie Kenny makes an impressive debut with this tale of lost innocence and pleasure gained through submission.